RENDEZVOUS
IN BAGHDAD

BEN SHELDON

RENDEZVOUS IN BAGHDAD

iUniverse, Inc.
Bloomington

Rendezvous in Baghdad

This is a work of fiction. All of the characters, names, incidents, organizations, and dialogue in this novel are either the products of the author's imagination or are used fictitiously.

iUniverse books may be ordered through booksellers or by contacting:

iUniverse
1663 Liberty Drive
Bloomington, IN 47403
www.iuniverse.com
1-800-Authors (1-800-288-4677)

ISBN: 978-1-4759-3677-3 (sc)
ISBN: 978-1-4759-3679-7 (e)
ISBN: 978-1-4759-3678-0 (dj)

Library of Congress Control Number: 2012912192

Printed in the United States of America

iUniverse rev. date: 9/12/2012

Chapter 1--Habemus Papam

(We Have A Pope)

THRONGS OF HUMANITY PACKED Rome's St. Peter's Square on this cool April morning, at the Vatican. They jostled, waited and waited, for a smoke signal from the chimney, above the Sistine Chapel. A groan went up, as a plume of smoke puffed out of the stack. It was black, telling the world that no pope was elected, with the cardinals' ballots, that just went ablaze in the conclave's fireplace. Outside, a baby cried, and its excited mother rattled, in fast Italian, with animated gestures. The baby mysteriously fell silent.

Watching the spectacle on television, from San Francisco, was Luke Godwin, a former seminary student, supervised by Father Paul Rogan, now Cardinal Rogan, presently ensconced in the Sistine Chapel, voting for the next pope. With an indelible smirk on his face, Luke made a clearing on the coffee table for snacks, prepared by Sami Yusuf, his Iraqi American lover. Both, now older and wiser, were young and attractive, when under Father Rogan's supervision.

"I hope he hasn't turned the conclave into an orgy!" remarked Luke with that sarcastic look, barely camouflaging his pained soul.

"You mean son-of-a-dog Rogan," responded Sami; "that Baghdad Jesuit, who decided celibacy was optional!" he added, straightening his US Air Force shirt.

"You're insulting man's best friend," Luke shot back. Sami quickly explained that he fell in the Baghdad custom of swearing, wherein son-of-a-dog was more derogatory than son-of-a-bitch.

In Rome, another black stream spun out of Sistine's chimney, as the hushed masses stretched their necks for a look at the dark smoke. So did Luke and Sami, watching the TV screen in Luke's condominium, that overlooked the Golden Gate bridge.

"Quite a sexual trek for a priest, from Baghdad to San Francisco, and still a well-kept secret?!" wondered Sami.

"Not sure about that; you and I know. But who'll believe us? Priests who know, hide the hot potato in their own closets, and stay silent," said Luke, munching on crackers.

Suddenly, white smoke spiraled out of the Sistine roof, and a great roar went up from the huge crowd on the Vatican grounds. The TV camera briefly focused on Sister Serena of East Timor. She jumped on an old rickety chair, near the Basilica steps, shouting: "E bianco, it's definitely white!" Looking at her fellow Silesian Sisters, she cheered: "Viva Il Papa!" Moments later, the bells of St. Peter's rang, confirming the election of the new pontiff.

All eyes now shifted to the Basilica's curtain-draped central balcony, that overlooked St. Peter's Square. Several minutes later, an eternity to the outside masses, the balcony doors swung open. Heinrich Dengler, the rotund dean of the College of Cardinals, stepped out to face a wildly cheering crowd below. Red cap shimmering in the bright sun, the normally-stern head cardinal forced a smile from his round face, as he declared to those below, and the world beyond:

"Habemus Papam!"

The TV anchorman wasted no time in translating from Latin: "We have a Pope."

Luke had bet Sami that the new pope would have to be tough Cardinal Heinrich Dengler. He would have cleaned up the Catholic Church from scandalous sexual priests. Sami placed his two dollars on Iraqi Cardinal Samuel Bidawid. It was obvious to him that the conclave would go in the direction of the Third World, to stem the tide of Islam. What better way than an Arab pope, similar to the Polish one who brought down the godless communist empire. In St. Peter's Square, the cheering and clapping reached a deafening crescendo, as Dengler ushered the new pope onto the balcony.

"I present to you Pope Urban IX, you know as cardinal Paul Rogan," announced the leader of the College of Cardinals.

Wearing a white cassock and skull cap, former Father Paul Rogan moved to the edge of the balcony. A red cape covered his shoulders, and an embroidered stole was at his neck. The new Holy Father addressed the sea of well-wishers in the square below, as Luke and Sami watched on TV, in San Francisco. Many knelt there in the huge Vatican hard ground, boasting as the first souls to be blessed by the new pope.

"Dear brothers and sisters, after the great Pope, who was just recalled by the Lord, the cardinals have elected me--a simple, humble shepherd, to help guide His flock," said the Pope.

"And molest His unsuspecting sheep!" added Luke, stunned at this papal selection.

For several minutes after, Luke and Sami were speechless, staring at each other. Then Sami took a deep breath, hugged Luke, and picked up some cups and dishes.

"He's not gonna get away with what he did to you!" said Sami, shuffling dispiritedly to the kitchen.

"What about his Arabian Nights with you at Baghdad Jesuit high?!" replied Luke, rolling his blue eyes upwards.

"That was a long time ago--before Iraq's government took over that school, sending their celibate and promiscuous priests packing to their sponsoring college, in Boston," shouted Sami from the kitchen, between sounds of clinking crockery and a whooshing faucet. But it all was soon drowned out by the cheering on TV. It emanated from Rome, during Pope Urban IX blessing of the ocean of humanity in the vast piazza. Sami emerged from the kitchen, wiping his tan face and patting down the curly black hair. Once again he was transfixed on the television screen.

"Looks like crime pays doubly," said Luke, jerking his head from the TV, towards Sami, his blond hair shifted vigorously from side to side; "once by the church, then again by this ignorant adoring public." Luke pointed two fingers at Sami, then one finger at the new pope. The only consolation they felt, on this April Fools' Day, was that it could be a farce, cooked up by the TV station. Recalling an old BBC-TV April lie, Sami described how the fake documentary depicted Italians harvesting spaghetti from trees.

"Did you know that Pope Urban II started the crusade wars against the Muslims?" Luke recalled from his seminary classes.

"Great! Now he'll have the Islamists after his ass," said Sami.

4

The Pontiff acknowledged the shouts of "Viva Il Papa" and a myriad hands, waving like stalks in a vast cornfield. Gracefully turning around, the brand new Holy Father walked off the papal balcony into a new Catholic era.

Chapter 2--A Question Of Honor

LUKE AND SAMI WERE asleep on the couch, in front of the TV, for quite sometime after the new pope had been elected. A doorbell sound in a TV ad awoke Luke. It was past midnight. He gently poked Sami into consciousness.

"Hadn't you better go back to the base, Sami. You're almost AWOL," smiled Luke.

"They gave me a few days off. My brother is visiting from Iraq," Sami replied with a wide-mouthed yawn. Luke proceeded to put new sheets and pillowcases on the bed, as Sami picked up a nearby Bay Area Reporter, a free-circulation gay newspaper. He flipped through it, to the advertising section. A little later, Luke joined him on the couch.

"I hope you don't take gay magazines and papers to the base," laughed Luke.

"They don't ask, I don't tell," Sami shot back with a mischievous smile.

"Is that why you let Rogan--pardon me, the Pope!--get away with what he did to you, Sami?" Luke said with a loving concern on his face. Sami scratched his forehead and burrowed his butt deeper into the cushion, trying to avoid an answer. Then he turned the tables on Luke, asking him why he had done nothing about Rogan's sexual abuse.

"I was here on a green card, serving in a homophobic military. What is your excuse?" asked Sami, mussing Luke's blond hair. He had peered over to see the ad that Sami spotted in the Reporter. He read, audibly: "young white top male, 300 pounds, seeking trim blond guy for long term relationship." Sami suggested that Luke grab this man, before Sami's rumored transfer to Europe. With a loud chuckle, Luke recommended that the fat man move overseas with Sami, as a team to climb the Alps. In a desperately lonely place, any kind of friend would be better than none, Luke elucidated.

Conversation then shifted to the itinerary of Sami's brother. Luke offered that both stay here in his condominium, saving the two expensive San Francisco hotels. But Sami's hesitation troubled Luke, who demanded to know why he could not do this little favor for his bosom buddy, if not soul mate.

"Dragging you into a cultural quagmire, is the last thing I want to do to you, my dear Luke," said Sami putting his dovetailed hands over his head.

Luke really wanted to know. Being late into the night, Sami tried to summarize it, as though his car was double-parked. Demands of his Air Force boss was weighing on his mind.

"It's all about a Muslim's honor" said Sami.

"Are you suggesting that Christians have no honor?" retorted Luke.

"I'm talking about a type of shame that's a death sentence in a Muslim family, " Sami shifted, looked down then up. Puzzled, Luke admitted that he did not really know what Sami was talking about. He kept asking anyway.

"So if I'm a Muslim and fuck another man, the law orders my execution?" asked Luke, eyes rolling up.

"No, not if you're fucking. But if you've ever been fucked, your brother, father or a close family member must kill you. It's the only way to restore family honor," replied Sami hesitantly.

At this point, Luke jumped out of the couch fuming. He told Sami in a loud voice that his society was so primitive, it was not even funny. How could he tolerate such a barbaric double standard.

"Hey, don't get mad at me! I didn't invent it. Why do you think I'm in San Francisco?" Sami fidgeted.

Calming down, Luke gazed into Sami's eyes and apologized for adding to his grief. However, he emphasized that if Sami's brother ever tried to kill Sami, then Luke himself would have to shoot him first--honor or no Muslim honor! But Sami instantly assured him that he was very close to his brother, Jamal. He was never violent. Then Luke renewed the invitation to him and his brother to stay in his condominium, vowing to keep mum about their gay relationship. That way Luke would not be interrogated as to who was 'top' or 'bottom'--the latter being a deadly male no-no, in Muslim culture.

The two lovers retired for the night, in agreement on that crucial Iraqi cultural caveat, and what to reveal to Sami's relatives.

Chapter 3--Visitor From Baghdad

IT WAS A LITTLE past noon, when the Airbus touched down at San Francisco International airport. Sami watched the accordion-shaped walkway being attached to the plane. He waved at aircraft windows, in case Jamal could see him. Finally the stream of passengers started entering the terminal, from the attached pathway. In the event his brother had changed his appearance or clothes, Sami examined every passenger as soon as each one got into view. There was a sturdy lad holding a bible. Smiling, Sami shook his head in the negative. More passengers streamed in. Behind a fat woman in tight pants was an old man, with a walking stick. Laughing, Sami muttered: "definitely not him!" Then Sami spotted Jamal, carrying the blue Pierre Cardin carry-on bag he had given him, a few birthdays ago.

"Welcome to Baghdad-by-the-Bay," said Sami, rushing to Jamal with open arms.

"The one I left behind must be Baghdad-by-the-Desert!" Jamal chuckled. The two kissed on each cheek, with Sami stooping a little.

"Hey, you're still shorter, despite eating more than me!" said Sami, as he hugged Jamal. Giggling audibly, the two marched off to the baggage-claim carousel. To Sami's surprise, Jamal picked up just one bag. It seemed odd, having come for a long stay. Soon they were all loading up into Sami's ten-year old Escort wagon. Seeing it in Sami's eyes, Jamal explained that he could not be candid, speaking from Iraq. All the phone lines were routinely tapped by Iraq's Mukhabarat Intelligence and US terrorist hunters. He would never have got a US visa, humping large suitcases, looking like an immigrant, while waving a temporary permit.

"Then you're here for good!" beamed Sami. Jamal sighed and wished he could work.

They won't let him on his student visa. At post-college age, Jamal was not sure what he was going to study. For sure he was not returning to Iraq. If it meant spending ten years in America, to disprove Einstein's theory of relativity, then so be it, he told Sami.

"Well, he's the one Jew you cannot make a fool of. Pick on another, like Freud--maybe not; if you can figure him out, I'll know for sure you're crazy!" said Sami laughing. He then asked Jamal if he was hungry. With the Muslim fasting month of Ramadan starting the following day, Jamal wanted to eat all day today. Sami nodded, and drove straight to downtown San Francisco. As the hills popped up in front of them, Jamal's face lit up.

"I thought Istanbul was the ultimate in beauty. This town beats it by a mile!" said Jamal. Sami told him he had not seen anything yet. They traveled through busy Market street to its dead end, got off, and walked into the Hyatt Regency, for lunch. Jamal tried to figure out how they had created the great outdoors, all indoors. There was a complete brook, flowing near the spacious lounging area, where they took up a table.

A rocket-shaped elevator suddenly crawled up an external wall. Jamal was taken aback, aborting Sami's attempt to catch the attention of a waitress.

"Why are you jittery? You're no longer in Iraq!" said Sami sympathetically.

"Reminds me of the Iran war, when one of their rockets-- looking like that--fell on an apartment building in Mansur, one block from home. It shook our house like it was a giant crib." Jamal pulled a paper tissue. "After a long while, I climbed out of the basement and went outside," he wiped his moist eyes, as Sami stared:

"What did you see?" he asked

"A vacant lot, with my best friend, Nabil, buried in it!" Jamal noticed that his audience was quietly enraptured. He felt free to complete the catharsis of this bottled up tragedy. His friend's parents survived. They were visiting at a qabool. This monthly open home was an old Baghdad tradition for family friends. They soon moved to Dora, till recently driven out by Sunni armed men, cleansing the mixed neighborhood of Shiites, like Nabil and his family. Jamal sobbed. Changing the atmosphere, Sami took Jamal to see some of the sights, which Sami had written his brother about. Suddenly Jamal shouted:

"There's your postcard!" pointing at the low layer of fog around the towers of the Golden Gate bridge. Sami nodded in a quiet smile, as he moved on to a zigzagging street. Again Jamal would scream with delight: "There's another one: the Crookedest Street in the World!" Sami was so glad to see Jamal happy, after all these years of wartime misery and deprivation in Iraq. There were a couple more postcards Jamal wanted to check out: Fishermen's Wharf and Alcatraz. Sami was very obliging; anything less and Jamal would revert to his hometown depression.

There would be one additional stop that was not in the postcards, that Jamal had received from Sami.

Chapter 4--Culture Shock

"WHAT! A STREET NAMED for Fidel Castro?!" exclaimed Jamal.

"No, it's what they call the gay district of San Francisco, and it's definitely not to honor Fidel," replied Sami cautiously.

"So everybody must be happy here; I'll smile too," Jamal chuckled.

"No, no; not everyone is happy here. In fact some are plain miserable. I'll explain to you later," replied Sami in a reflective mood. He continued on to Luke's condominium. Sami knocked on the door lightly, so as not to awaken Luke, should he be asleep. After one minute of wait, Sami opened the door with his own key, as the two brothers tiptoed in. They shed their extra garments, washed up and then relaxed, viewing the Golden Gate bridge.

There was some clicking at the bedroom door. It swept open, and a man in Saddam Hussein mask walked into the living room. Startled, Jamal half-stood up, not knowing what to do. Sami told his brother to sit and calm down, as he admonished his friend for poor taste.

"Honestly Luke, my brother runs away from one dictator, only to run into another here; take the mask off and meet my kid brother," Sami rose introducing the two.

Jamal embraced, the Iraqi way, with a traditional Middle Eastern kiss on each cheek, then sat down again. Luke reminded Sami that it was Halloween today. He then asked if they celebrated it in Iraq.

"Does he mean Ashura," Jamal turned to Sami, who chuckled loudly, looking at the puzzled Luke.

"I assure you, it's fun," Luke chimed in, ignorant of what Iraq's Ashura celebration was about.

He wanted to know their little private joke. Sami went on to explain that it had some similarities to Halloween, with a difference. Instead of a mask, they would totally hide behind a pushiya, a black veil over the face, and an abaya, a long loose black outer garment. They then would go door to door asking for goodies, much like here. Any attempt to unveil a face, could result in a sharp pinprick on the host's buttock, elaborated Sami.

"Then your Assure-ya, or whatever you call your Iraqi Halloween, is just for veiled women?" Luke wanted to know. Chuckling, Sami was eager to elucidate. By custom, no one would talk from inside this perfect cover-up, Sami explained. Hence, men have been known to don women's pushiyas and abayas, then go knocking on doors for gifts, during the night of Ashura, not 'Assure-ya', he emphasized." He'll see the difference between Iraqi Halloween and ours for himself tonight," Luke handed the mask to Jamal, who quickly set it aside, out of view, and forced a polite smile.

Sami pulled Luke aside, and told him that he had not come out to his brother, about being gay. That it was not appropriate to drag Jamal to such a campy event. Luke retorted that sooner or later Jamal would find out. What better way than to let him know in this festive atmosphere.

"It'll all be just too funny to be mad at a gay brother," whispered Luke, mussing Sami's hair.

From the closet, Luke pulled out some masks, a Roman toga, straw halos, a witch's hat and other paraphernalia, then dumped them all on the couch; "take your picks," he invited the brothers, "I'll be a former Iraqi president--say, Saddam Hussein. You can be a former U.S. Presidents," said Luke, pointing to masks of Clinton, Nixon, Carter and the two Bushes, calling them George the First and Second. Jamal rummaged through them, vacillating between awe and embarrassment.

"In Iraq, we've been nothing for years, and you're asking me to be President of the United States!" said Jamal, rather amused.

Peeking into the closet again, Luke brought out a Kissinger and a Bin Laden mask. He threw them on the couch. Sami interjected, explaining to Jamal. Though it was not an Iraqi custom to wear masks, here it was done in fun. He urged Jamal to pick something, so as not to look strangely normal in public. Jamal picked up George I mask and dumped it: "He killed many people, when bombing Baghdad," he mumbled in Arabic to his brother. George II mask was rejected, as perpetuating the bombings and killings in Iraq. Jamal smiled at Carter and Clinton masks: "I like them, but these make them look like clowns," said Jamal, as if talking to himself. Kissinger's mask was shoved aside decisively enough for Luke to notice.

"He's a Jew!" retorted Jamal.

Luke asked if Arabs were anti-Semitic. Sami barged in to explain that Arabs were Semitic too. Both races descended from the Prophet Abraham. But all Jews were virtual Israelis, through Israel's Law of Return. It conferred on any Jew the Israeli citizenship, just for the asking.This empowered them to settle in confiscated Arab lands.

"So how can an Arab be anti-himself?!" added Sami rhetorically.

Finally, Jamal chose the Nixon mask. He explained, that though he was president, Nixon left the White House sad, broken and unloved. Jamal was experiencing a similar tragedy--ejected from home. Sami donned the straw halo, and slipped into the Roman toga, the nearest look-alike to an Iraqi dishdasha, worn by men. The halo seemed like the kaffiyeh Arab headdress, to Sami. It felt comfortable and homey.

Everyone was now ready to hit town, on this Halloween night.

Chapter 5--Confessional Halloween

DOWNSTAIRS, LUKE USHERED THE two chatty brothers into the back of his red convertible. He knew that they still had plenty to talk about, and in a language, totally unintelligible to him. This was no Spanish; not even Cantonese. Luke had picked up a few words in both languages from college friends. So he settled for the sole role of chauffeur, since he was not going to catch one word from Jamal's conversation with Sami.

Jumping behind the steering wheel, he pressed a button, sending the convertible top upwards and over their heads. Jamal objected. He had seen Hollywood movie stars, with their hair blowing, while riding in red convertibles. He wanted to find out how it felt. Sami interjected.

"This Baghdad-by-the-Bay is much colder than your Baghdad by the desert, that you happily left behind; it's colder than even Hollywood!" Sami showed off his superior knowledge to his younger brother. "Remember the Mark Twain lesson at Baghdad Jesuit high? He said: "the coldest winter I experienced, was a summer in San Francisco!" Sami added. Jamal laughed politely, and agreed to postpone the Hollywood open-top experience.

Being still early for real Halloween action, Luke just drove around the tourist attractions of San Francisco, starting at Fishermen's Wharf. Every now and then, Luke would notice a lull in the chatter, as the two brothers paused. They would pop their heads up to take in the bright lights, then sink back into homesick gabbing. He quit listening to that foreign yakking.

But it was serious gossip from home, about cousin Najma, who had an eye for Sami when he left for America. Luke quickly added 'Najma' to his limited Arabic vocabulary, after Sami explained that it meant 'star' in Iraq. Rumors had swirled in social circles, that she had sex with a lout, thus besmirching the respected family name. To salvage their reputation, her brother killed her, to restore the family honor, as required by custom and culture. The perpetrator spent six months in jail, in conformity with the law that frowned at loose women. Sami was visibly upset, because he was fond of his cousin.

"Here, if one kills even some useless whore, the government may kill the killer; or send him somewhere like that," Sami pointed at an Alcatraz poster, "before the prison was closed." Below the sign, at Pier 39 complex, stood a line of tourists, waiting for the Alcatraz ferry.

"Age-old traditions, like chastity, commanded by the Holy Quran, have also prevented ancient and modern plagues, like AIDS, according to the mullah's sermon," Jamal eyed Luke, explaining that 'mullah' was a Muslim cleric, equivalent to a priest or minister.

They got off at Pier 39, with its array of restaurants, cafes, exhibits and the games pavilion. Luke went to throw a few balls inside the pavilion. The two brothers continued their reminiscences in a cafe, over tea and baqlava, their favorite pastry back home.

"So men can screw around with women, as well as men; the ladies get killed, but the guys get off smelling like a rose," sighed Sami.

"Not all of them; men who get screwed by other men, go the way of the sluts," replied Jamal.

"Even if the fucker is the Pope?" asked Sami, looking serious.

"Now that's really funny. You still come up with off-the-wall jokes!" chuckled Jamal.

"If you found out in Baghdad that a close relative of yours was screwed by a priest, would you kill your kinfolk or the priest?" asked Sami with a straight face. Jamal sought a little crack of a smile, but there was none. Then Luke barged in, all smiles, carrying a stuffed teddy bear that he had won, inside the games' pavilion.

They pushed the new furry passenger into the car. They all followed in and drove off to Baghdad Café. It was on Market street, a few blocks from Castro street. Jamal smiled broadly at the joint's name-- proud that his hometown was commemorated so far away. It was spacious with high, wide windows, overlooking the city's main thoroughfare. Facing the entrance, in his wheelchair at a strategic table, was Clive. He was a bulky middle-aged gay flirt, with a handsome face and remnants of two flimsy legs. Noisily he waved at Luke and Sami and winked. Close by, he shook hands, then crawled his palms up and down Luke's bare arm. He started on Sami, who demurely, pulled back. He glance at his brother, with some embarrassment. Luke explained to Jamal that Clive thought he was in love with every cute guy in The City. Nonchalant, Clive introduced the two young handsome men flanking him, as though members of his male harem. Soon, Clive's two acquaintances left for

21

greener pastures in fertile gay bars. Sensing the tenseness between Jamal and Sami, Luke tried to change the subject. Clive attributed his audacity to his mother, who had always treated him as a normal son. Hence he never acted as an invalid.

"So how many gay Jehovah's Witnesses did you snatch from the Sunday service?" Luke asked Clive. He had been a Witness for years. Upon discovering he was gay, they kicked him out. Ever since, it became a personal crusade to ferret out gay Jehovah's Witnesses. He wanted to rescue them from that church, through leaflets, pickets and other means.

"Well, we saved two souls this week," Clive replied. "they were cute too," he beamed. Jamal nudged at Sami, who pulled on Luke's sleeve, and the three left. They walked into Castro street. It had been blocked off to traffic, along with the surrounding streets. By now, Castro was filled wall-to-wall with revelers, in carnival mood, and dressed in every imaginable costume. Jamal pointed at some nuns, stating that he did not realize that this Halloween was some kind of a religious festival, like the Eid back home.

"Take it from me, Jamal, it is not religious. These are the Sisters-of-Nonstop-Indulgence; their bible is not the New Testament. It's quite something else!" said Luke, with a fertive wink at Sami. He did not wish to explain further to his puzzled brother. Half-naked men hand in hand, followed the nuns. This made even less sense to Jamal. Although he felt pushing it, Sami was almost ready to come out to his brother, as they strolled on, in this gay Mecca. Jamal stayed dazzled and confused, when entering the Cock 'N Bull dancing club. A drag queen at the bar reviewed the trio, then approached Jamal for a dance. Sami stepped in between, whispering into her ear: "He has carpal tunnel syndrome; take him; he's hot!" and pulled Luke by the hand and gently shoved him against the dumbfounded drag queen. Her hair plumage vibrated over the tall wig. Luke played along, pulling her to the dance floor.

"Isn't she gorgeous?!" said Jamal.

"Yes, but you wouldn't want to marry her," Sami replied, turning his smirk toward the dance floor. He then dragged Jamal to a calmer corner, where he could hear himself talk. He quietly told Jamal that he was the dearest family member. That is why he could no longer deceive him. In an embarrassed whisper, Sami told him that he was gay, and had always been that way.

"So that's why you did not marry," recalled Jamal. Sami concurred. "You know Mama used three matchmakers for months, till they came up with the daughter of Rashad. He was Mosul's former mayor, who was Baba's best friend--no doubt you still remember," Jamal recalled, nostalgically. Rashad felt slighted and was never close to father again, Jamal added. Sami nodded pensively, resigned to something he had no control over. To cheer up Sami, Jamal explained that it was really no big deal being a "boy seeker" over there, as long as one got married and produced grand kids for the parents.

"I could not get married to anyone," said Sami nervously moving his glass back and forth.

"But why? Everyone does it all over the Middle East." Jamal very much wanted Sami to get grandchildren for mother's sake, especially when Jamal himself was infertile. In fact, to make his absence palatable to Mama, Jamal promised he would do his best to bring back Sami, so he could marry the wonderful new young lady she had found for him. Jamal was so persistent, that he forced Sami's hand right then and there.

"Jamal, I could not tell this to Mama, but I must tell you, so you'll understand once and for all. I am a boy seeker; they call it gay, here. We are in the Castro district of San Francisco; it is the boy-seekers capital of America. Those were not nuns; they were men in nun's clothes," Sami wanted to go on but paused, seeing a tear roll down Jamal's cheek.

"How can I tell Mama she can never have a grandson?" Jamal breathed deeply."Even if I could get married, I cannot go back and face Baba?" mumbled Sami as if to himself, but Jamal heard him anyway.

"Father has nothing against you. I don't understand," Jamal moved in his seat.

Tears streaming down his eyes, Sami told Jamal that he could not face Baba until he had cleansed out a shame, which was perpetrated against him some years ago at Baghdad Jesuit highschool. Jamal pressed him for more details, but Sami could not bear to go into it any further. Luke laughed on hearing the word Baba, having recently seen Ali Baba and the Forty Thieves. Jamal had to explain that 'Baba' was Baghdadi for 'dad'.

"I have an old account to settle with the new Pope, before I can see Baba," Sami picked up a paper tissue and wiped around his eyes. Jamal thought that Sami was losing touch with reality and himself.

Luke slipped away then returned, dragging a young guy in Arab headdress. Quickly, Sami put the pope's miter on his head, as Jamal wore Jimmy Carter's mask.

"Meet his Holiness. He's already forgiven me as the Butcher of Baghdad," said Luke introducing his new friend to Sami. They laughed, as they jostled their way out of the club, exchanging sharp repartees.

Chapter 6--Short Sojourn

BACK AT THE CONDO, Luke pulled a roller-bed out of the closet for Jamal. Sami chose the couch for himself, instead of the double-bed that he would normally share with Luke. It was a cultural concession to Jamal. It would avoid the honor question, as to who did anal sex to whom. This arrangement would be repeated three more nights. By then, Sami's special Air Force leave would expire.

During this short time off, Sami took his brother to Jamal's favorite spots. It turned out to be places of genuine Middle Eastern cuisine, especially gyros, dolmas, kabobs and the rare kubba. It had to be topped off with baqlava. But none compared with their mother's cooking and dessert. They sorely missed that je-ne-sais-quoi element, which Mama added to the recipe.

All the while Jamal was quietly deciding where to live, during his US sojourn, pending a final status. He aimed at a permanent residency in America, fulfilling a lifelong dream. It started when he saw New York flaunting its tall buildings on a wall poster of a Baghdad travel agency. This was in the good old days when Iraqis could travel, with few obstacles. He knew no one in New York City, but would settle for Tampa Bay, Florida.

It was the adopted home of Uncle Mahzoom--the name being an Iraqi epithet, meaning runaway.

In the brothers' final night in Luke's condo, there were fond conscious farewells to preempt the sleepy morning goodbyes. Luke then got into his striped red and black pajamas, while Sami stayed in underwear. Luke stared at Jamal's night outfit and whispered to Sami:

"What's with your straight brother; why is he in drag?"

"That's the dishdasha, our traditional male night dress," Sami laughed out loud. Jamal told Luke that he had brought an extra one as a gift. He offered it to Luke, for being a good host, as well as looking after his brother.

"It's great for next year's Halloween," Luke accepted with a chuckle. His shy cat, Cardinal, sneaked in and rubbed against Jamal's leg.

"Cardinal for a cat's name?" muttered Jamal. Luke pointed to the feline's reddish fur on the head.

"Notice his red holy cap!" Luke smiled, then excused himself to go watch his TV favorite program, in the bedroom.

Sami made chamomile tea, as Mama used to, especially when they had the sniffles. On a small plate, he placed some kulach, which they got from a Lebanese deli. Its baked dough was stuffed with a mixture of nuts and sugar in some, and mashed pitted dates in others. It was Jamal's favorite pastry back home, especially at the end of the daily Ramadan fast. The two munched and sipped tea, while hunched over a low glass table. The large living room window framed San Francisco's skyline and the Golden Gate bridge.

"I come all the way to America to see you, and they send you all the way to Italy," said Jamal ruefully.

"Trust them to transfer me to northern Italy, not far from Rome. How can I rest in peace knowing that the holy pedophile is holed up in the Vatican!" Sami lay down hard his istikan, a small Iraqi teacup, spilling some tea. Jamal urged him to relax, and not depress himself unnecessarily. "I must cleanse our honor, so I can face Baba again, before he's recalled by our Maker," said Sami in the Iraqi vernacular.

"Even in Iraq you cannot restore family honor by killing a molester, once they reach the status of a big shot. But a Pope? Heaven help us!" Jamal put his arm around Sami, then both rose to retire for the night. Jamal went to the rollaway bed, while Sami headed for the sofa bed.

In the morning, Luke rose first, got ready for work at the AIDS hospice, where he was a director. Before leaving, he brewed some coffee in a percolator, baked a frozen roll of biscuits. He played out loud a Sousa march, as they would on the base, to wake Sami and other service men, in a home-style reveille. Sami jumped to attention, saw Luke's sheepish grin, then relaxed, scratching his tummy. Jamal woke up sniffing fresh baking. It smelled just like the Baghdad summoon bread. For a second he thought he was back in Mansur. "I was gonna get you that donut," said Luke pointing to a fog ring around a tower of the Golden Gate bridge, "but it got too big!" He then hugged Jamal, who was on his way to the bathroom. Momentarily alone with Sami, Luke gave him a passionate kiss, and hoped to see him again as an Air Force General. He then left the two brothers behind in his condo.

To catch Jamal's plane to Florida, the two brothers took BART to San Francisco International airport. On the way, Sami fell in the old habit of giving unsolicited advice to his younger brother. It slipped his mind that Jamal had also matured into an adult. As usual, Jamal declared himself as a fully-grown man, and would have none of that haughty advice. By boarding time, the pair mellowed substantially, hugging goodbye with moist eyes.

The third man to depart, got on public transportation. It dropped him off at the Air Force base, where Sami reported for duty.

Chapter 7--Transfer Orders

EARLY NEXT MORNING, COLONEL Sami Yusuf was at his desk. He saw an urgent note from his superior, Brigadier General Paul Pachelli, who was also the Base Commander. Sami took a quick sip off his coffee--not exactly Starbucks Frappuccino flavor--then rushed over to Pachelli's office. He greeted the Brigadier General with his slightly shaky salute. Pachelli rose, shook his hand and seated him in the plush leather chair. He would normally offer that chair to the Major General and higher ranks.

"You're being transferred to my old country, Italy. That makes you a paisano!" said Pachelli, with a wistful smile. Sami moved his butt in the cushion and grinned back, as the general continued: "Did you know that pope Pius XII was Eugenio Pacelli,?"

"No, sir." Sami's head swiveled sideways.

"I just know Rogan is the new pope. I don't like him," added Sami.

Pachelli wondered why, but Sami just shrugged, mumbling that it was a long story. The general went on to explain that the Italian letter, c, in his famous granduncle's name was pronounced 'ch' in Italian, as in his own Americanized name. General Pachelli then pulled out a Chianti bottle from his bottom desk drawer, poured some of the Italian wine into a teacup, and then offered a drink to Colonel Yusuf. He politely demurred.

"Here's to the old country, and to the memory of a great pope!" Pachelli sipped from the teacup. "So humble he was, even when Pope, he'd answer the phone as Pacelli," said the brigadier general, handing colonel Sami Yusuf a Pepsi. The airman accepted it gratefully. He was a little uncomfortable with the non-military atmosphere, as if waiting for the other heavier shoe to drop. It did. "Now let's get down to business, I mean Air Force business." Pachelli rose, and walked over to a map of Italy on the wall. He pointed the tip of a long stick at the Air Force base.

"Aviano is way up here in northern Italy--lotsa mountains, and we have quite a base there, not far from the skiing areas. A while back, one of our pilots, in low-flight training, yanked out a cable, attached to some ski lift, which was moving a car-full of skiers," said the general. Sami dutifully put on a mask of horror, asking if any were injured. "Injured? Are you kidding! Dead; all dead," Pachelli poured some more Chianti wine, watching colonel Yusuf's face scrunch up some more. "This is where you come in. Your low-flying skills can be very valuable here. You will train our pilots for combat in mountainous trouble spots of the world," the General eagerly explained to a more relaxed Sami.

Distaff sergeant Cohen walked in and handed the base commander a bunch of papers. He kept some, and handed the rest to Sami.

"Here's detailed instructions on your transfer. Read them carefully and note down anything you do not understand, by this afternoon. Because tomorrow, my friend, you'll be over there, almost as good as Italiano!" sighed Pachelli. Colonel Yusuf got out of the comfortable chair, saluted, took the order file and marched out. He gently closed the door behind.

"Maybe I'm prejudiced, but I feel queasy about Arabs learning sophisticated flying techniques," said sergeant Cohen. The brigadier general admonished and reminded her that colonel Yusuf was an American just like her. The only difference being, she was Jewish American and he was Arab American. "I understand where you're coming from. You served in the Israeli Army; to you every Arab is a potential terrorist," said the tall general, looking down at the petite sergeant; "you still have that Middle East syndrome. In America, we're all equal citizens. In World War II, Italian Americans bombed Italy, as Americans," he opened a drawer and pulled out a file. He handed it to the sergeant, then continued: "Colonel Yusuf is a good American. End of speech. Thank you sergeant," said the base commander, picking up the phone. The sergeant saluted and walked out.

At his quarters, Sami was busy packing and filling brown bags with junk, destined for the dump. During a lull, he called Luke to tell him about his international itinerary. Flipping through the papers he had just received, Sami gave him the new address; he also promised to call in his new phone number from Italy. Luke wished to chat some more, but Sami had to go to a little farewell get-together, arranged by lieutenant Gallo. "You mean Oral, the Roman closet queen!" Luke laughed. Sami was not amused, explaining how great Oral had been helping him with many little things that Sami was too busy for, while getting ready for transfer to Italy. He added that Gallo came from a religious family, with many relatives still living near Rome.

"He was even named after evangelist Oral Roberts," said Sami.

"I would've given him the same name, but for a different reason!" Luke guffawed. Sami's forehead creased with a little frown. Luke apologized, then asked Sami how a Catholic, like Gallo, could be named after a protestant evangelist.

"Very simple. His mom is a Southern Baptist," said Sami, bidding his friend au revoir.

After the party, Sami had a long chat about Italy with lieutenant Oral Gallo. He gave Sami material about the great places to see, if he ever visited Rome on leave. Oral raved about the Vatican, and what to see there. He laid out a detailed map for it. He explained what to observe in Rome, when and where the Pope would show up, to bless the crowds in St. Peter's Square. Oral insisted that Sami keep the Vatican map, since he himself could get any information he might need, from his relatives. After all, they lived in Rome.

Despite all this frantic last minute activity, Sami was in bed by 10 p.m. He must be ready for a military flight that would depart the following morning, at 8 a.m. sharp.

Chapter 8--First Trip to Italy

IT WAS SUNNY WITH some haze, as the military transport plane flew over Venice, on its way to nearby Aviano airbase. Colonel Sami Yusuf looked down from the window, and noticed a grand palace. He surmised that it belonged to a powerful doge, who had ruled the great Venice, centuries ago. Could he have been the chief that financed the crusaders, who sacked Constantinople? Sami wondered. He had difficulty figuring out, how devout Christians on their way to save Jerusalem, would destroy the grandest Christian city of its era. Then he remembered reading that when the first crusaders, egged on by Pope Urban II, entered Jerusalem, they slaughtered every Muslim and Jewish inhabitant of the city.

"How could they do that, when Jesus preached love?!" colonel Yusuf mumbled to himself.

On the right was the blue Adriatic sea; below him, the pervasive Venice canals shimmered in the sun, which spotlighted tourists in gondolas. It reminded him of an old classic Egyptian recording called "Song of the Gondola", crooned by his childhood idol, Abdul Wahab--the then Bing Crosby of the Arab world. Though Egyptian, the singer was as popular in Iraq and the

Arab countries, as in Egypt itself. USAF Colonel Yusuf felt real homesick for Baghdad. He also knew that he could never visit home and face his dad. To be sexually dishonored is bad enough over there. Even worse, was for a Muslim to be sodomized by a Christian, and a priest at that. The culture there would prescribe death as a remedy. The only other way to restore his worth, the Iraqi way, would be by the death of the perpetrator. It would have been much easier if the culprit was still Father Rogan, SJ, which signified membership in the Society of Jesus. Now that he had been elected pope, he had the gall of choosing the papal name of Urban IX. No doubt, Sami thought, it was after Pope Urban II, who started the 200-year Crusade Wars against the Muslims, like himself. Helpless and depressed, Sami suddenly saw, below, the lush greenery of the Po river valley. He remembered, from his Geography class at Baghdad Jesuit high, how the valley crops and produce fed much of Italy. Then his roving mind focused on Father Rogan and his secret escapades at Sami's old school. His face wrinkled up, as if in pain. He recalled the events, which ensued after taking Rogan's English class. That's when Father Rogan would take a respite from his priestly vow of celibacy.

By now the Dolomite mountains were in partial view. In the spiel to ameliorate his transfer, Sami was told that here started the great Alps, hence the second name, Pre-Alp. It was a piece of geology he was not crazy about, while craving for the flatlands of Baghdad and the banks of the Tigris river. To Colonel Yusuf, it was just another mountain, to fly clear over. Low clouds loitered half way down the mountain in some areas, looking like an extension of the snow cap. Below that, were scattered haze and blue mountain sides. A busy ski resort came into view. Several ski lifts were moving on long lines of cable.

The pilot deliberately flew clear around the complex, avoiding a flyover. Presently, some red roofs came into view, as the plane approached the landing strip of Aviano airport. It eventually taxied past the Tower Loop Dispersal and stopped, not far from it.

Brigadier General Anthony Amal was there in person to greet his new pilots and crew.

"Welcome to the 16th Air Force and the 31st Fighter Wing," said the commander, extending a hand. Sami saluted, then shook the general's hand

"We could use your low-flying talents here, Colonel Yusuf," said General Amal.

"Yes sir," Sami saluted again, clicking his heels.

"Southern Region needs your old country know-how for flights over Iraq, from Incerlik base in Turkey," added the General.

"Na'am, I mean yes, Sir," said Sami, embarrassed at using the Arabic word for 'yes'.

"I got it in both languages. I served two years at the U.S. Central Command in Cairo," smiled General Amal.

"If I may be permitted, Amal is Arabic for 'hope'," said Sami, a little more relaxed. General Amal could not resist pursuing this.

"Actually our family's name was Amalfitano, from Amalfi, here in Italy," the general cheerfully elaborated. "At Ellis Island, my grandfather agreed to shorten it to 'Amal', at the suggestion of a Lebanese American official, who gave him the meaning," said General Amal, as some personnel fidgeted with impatience. "Granddad told my mother, he kept the name, because that was exactly why he had come to America, and perhaps you too," said the general.

"Yes sir, it's exactly that," Sami's tenseness melted away, as though he'd found a kindly father. Amal waved over one of his personnel.

"Sergeant Brain, take Colonel Yusuf to his quarters. Be sure he finds his way, to be in my office at 1500 hours," said the general, turning to Sami, "we got lots to talk about," he concluded.

They all made a stiff walk towards the main building, as an F-117 Stealth Fighter approached for a landing.

On the way to his room, Sami looked at the friendly face of the staff sergeant and politely said: "You must be smart, for a general to call you 'Brain'."

"Cuz my name is Brainerd," the sergeant laughed.

"How did you get a name like that?" Sami sneaked a look at his handsome face.

"I was born there, in Brainerd, Minnesota. Amal thinks all Minnesotans have lots of brain; so he calls me that. He don't ask why the 'Gaynor' surname, so I don't tell him," smiled Brain, looking at Sami, as if his mental radar, known as gaydar, in San Francisco, told him: "it's OK, he's one of us!"

"You're so honest, Brain; I'm gay too," whispered Colonel Yusuf.

"We should have fun, in a homophobic military, inside a homophobic Catholic country, where the priests have all the fun!" said Sergeant Brain, as he opened the door to Sami's new abode.

"Some day I'll tell you lots more about it," said Colonel Sami Yusuf. He walked in, winked at Brain, then slowly shut the door behind.

Chapter 9--In The Alps:
New Home, New Job

AT EXACTLY THREE O'CLOCK that afternoon, Colonel Yusuf was ushered into Headquarters by Staff Sergeant Brainerd Gaynor, who saluted, turned to leave, and closed the door behind. Sami sat tensely, until the brigadier general offered him a coke. He timidly agreed. The general closed off the one window to outside fresh air, then raised the heater's thermostat.

"It can get pretty nippy here in December." the general handed Sami the soda can. "Sorry, no straws or glasses. We're not budgeted like a Marriot hotel!" Amal laughed. "But we get other perks, like free college, health insurance, food, lodging--you name it!" he grinned, showing some tobacco stain. It did not, however, make a dent in the appearance of this swarthy, tall, tanned military man.

"Did you see ski lifts and cables from the plane on your way here?" General Amal looked seriously at Colonel Yusuf.

"I sure did, Sir. I thought it would be fun on my day off," said Sami.

"That's the ski resort of Cavalese. We'll make sure what happened in Cavalese, never takes place here!" the general pounded the table gently. Colonel Yusuf remembered reading about it in San Francisco--a world away from the Dolomite mountains. He asked General Amal what exactly happened.

"A Marine Prowler surveillance plane flying way below the 500 feet limit, sheared cable car wires, sending a cabin hurtling to the frozen mountain side," said the general. Colonel Yusuf gasped. "That's not all; twenty skiers from several countries were crushed to death in the twisted metal of the cabin, "the general gulped down some whiskey from a disguised canteen. Sami wanted to know what was a Marine plane doing here, in Air Force country. "They belonged to a squadron based in Cherry Point, North Carolina, " Dwight Amal smirked. "What do you expect from yokels of Cherry Point, Nowhere Carolina!" General Amal laughed, then continued: "As a result, the Italians raised the minimum altitude for low-level flights from five hundred to two thousand feet, over the Italian Alps." The general looked out of the window, pointing at a similar twin-engine electronics warfare plane, just landing. "The Cherry Point dummies came and went, leaving us with lousy height limits. Even over the plains, south of these mountains, we must now fly at no less than a thousand feet, where we could train at five hundred feet." The general looked straight at Colonel Sami Yusuf; "and this is where your expertise comes in. We cannot afford to make one more mistake in low-flying exercises, or we'll face impossible altitudes, or worse--being thrown out by the Italians," said General Dwight Amal. The two watched another plane land. "We're proud of the Joint Strike Fighter. Have you flown a JSF?" asked the brigadier general.

"Yes, Sir. You name it, I've flown it," said Colonel Yusuf, exuding pride in his accomplishments.

"That's why you are here. Soon after the accident, I sent word to find the best, most versatile pilot, to train our flyers at low altitudes, with a hundred and ten percent safety!" smiled the general, proud of his find. Sami inquired as to why low flying was needed, since stealth planes could do it at any altitude.

"In some situations, where all our stealth craft are busy, we may still need low flights for certain missions." He pulled a drawer and took out photos of the ski resort accident. Colonel Yusuf stared at the messy cables and crushed ski cabin. His mouth stayed open like he had lockjaw.

"Sir, if I may say so, there's absolutely no excuse for this," the colonel handed back the pictures with a stunned look on his face.

"Now you know why you are in the Dolomite alps of Northern Italy." General Amal put the photos back in the drawer and locked it.

Colonel Sami Yusuf recommended that initial near-terrain flying be done above flat surface, like offshore waters. If the adjacent Adriatic sea provided insufficient surface, the wide waters beyond Venice or Tyrrhenian Sea, off Rome, would allow for plenty of flying space. General Amal was cool to that, especially after the Cavalese cable-car fiasco.

"It's not good public relations to interrupt the Holy Father in prayer, as planes leave the sea, and zoom over," said General Amal.

"From my personal knowledge of holy people, they don't always spend their time praying. They have fun too," said Sami, "sometimes too much fun," he added.

"Well, that's something else; none of our business. It's between them and God," the general rolled his eyes upward. Looking at Sami's dossier, he spotted his school record at Baghdad Jesuit high. "That's interesting; how did a Muslim end up at a Catholic school?" Dwight Amal looked at the colonel. Sami explained that his dad sent him to the best school he could find in Iraq; the Jesuit institution was that one.

Brigadier General Amal wound up the meeting, by handing Colonel Yusuf detailed orders, to be carried out, starting the following day. "Airman Roman Gallo is assigned to assist you," concluded the general.

Chapter 10--Aviano: Roman-born Airman Assists

NEXT MORNING, SAMI HAD breakfast with Gallo, to get acquainted and discuss preliminary matters. The colonel wondered how an American came to be named 'Roman'.

"I was born in Rome, the real one, not the little dinky town in Georgia!" Roman snickered. "My parents moved to San Francisco when I was ten. "Roman spread butter on an English muffin. Feeling like kin, also from the Bay Area, Sami asked where in the City did he grow up.

"Little Italy, of course--North Beach," Roman took a bite off the muffin. Nostalgically, Sami recalled buying Dragula from City Lights book store, on Halloween, and trying to read it in other hangouts. Roman remembered his dad talking about Carol Doda, and the big stink this first topless dancer caused in San Francisco, the state and prudish USA, way back when. The two had more than that in common; both had tan complexions and black hair. Roman was a little taller. Sami was dying to know the sexual orientation of this attractive guy, especially when he was not wearing a ring on the marked finger.

"Are you married?" Sami asked sheepishly.

"Sort of; you know, married with no formal paper work," grinned Roman. His wife was born and bred in Rome, he added. "Her folks are still in Rome, so she spends her time half there, half here," Gallo waved his hand back and forth.

"Perhaps some of our training missions can extend to Rome. You can visit the wife or her folks, during stopover," said Colonel Yusuf, with a pensive look on his face.

"That would be quite a surprise to just drop on them one day," Roman smiled broadly. "So don't get bored by yourself, I can show you the sights of the Eternal City, as they like to call it," said Gallo. Sami's face lit up.

"I'd love to see the Vatican." Sami got spirited.

"Hey, I know that cottage, like the back of my hand," Roman chuckled. "An uncle of mine was a priest. I'm tellin' ya, he knew people real close to the Pope. I almost met the Holy Father myself," said the airman, feeling important. This time Sami did not ask his favorite question: whether his uncle had fun as a priest!

The breakfast drinks dwindled towards the cups' bottoms, before realizing they had business to discuss. Roman pulled out some papers and maps from a brief case. Seeing that the dining room table was not appropriate to lay out paper work, Colonel Sami Yusuf asked if there was a good place to lay all this out. Airman Roman Gallo lead him to a conference room with a long wide table. Spread out over it, were topographic maps of Italy, Southern Europe, and the Middle East.

"You know, we can start out over sea surface; that's also equivalent to flying low over a desert too," the colonel said, authoritatively. "We can then progress to rugged and mountainous terrain, between here and Rome," he looked at

Roman and winked. Gallo understood it meant a visit to his folks, or the wife, if she was there too. Roman smiled back: "Yes sir, Colonel," he clicked his heels and saluted. Sami laughed: "you may relax, Airman," he said.

Colonel Yusuf scrutinized the topography around the Cavalese skiing area. He asked Roman if he had visited the accident scene.

"I sure did, even before they pulled out the mangled bodies. It was some scene," said Airman Gallo, overcome by deep thought.

"What are all these crossed-out numbers on the map?" Sami pointed to the accident site.

"They are the minimum altitudes before the Cavalese accident. The Italian government doubled that height on us, up here over our mountains," said Gallo.

"I see; so the numbers in ink, are the new minimum heights allowed." Sami moved the pointer between Venice and Rome areas. "Interesting terrain variations. I'd like to check it out, and select possible training regions," said the Colonel. "Here's Cavalese-- about a hundred miles northwest of Venice. That makes it pretty close to us, just a little farther west by north than Cavallejo..." Sami was interrupted by Roman.

"You mean Cavalese," he said.

"Close enough; when you've been to Frisco-Bay's cow town of Vallejo, as many times as I have, your tongue cannot escape it!" Sami Yusuf smiled.

"I remember Vallejo as a gambling bus stop on the way to Reno," said Roman; "I should have got off and shopped in that mega-village, instead of losing my shirt in Nevada," reminisced Airman Gallo. "By the way, don't ever say 'Frisco' in San Francisco!" Gallo added.

Concluding the meeting, Colonel Yusuf stipulated that the final ground-hugging lesson would require the plane to carry ordnance. This would test cockpit controls, under a heavy payload, to simulate a real-time sortie.

On the way out they chatted personal stuff. Gallo's wife was currently in Rome with her family, for a couple more months. Sami wanted to know if it bored him living here. How did people have fun in the boondocks?

"You can be a Hasher, like me, or a Bass Buster," Airman Gallo guffawed, reading zeros on Colonel Yusuf's face.

"Let's get together on Friday for dinner and a drink; that will give us enough time for you to explain this gibberish," Sami rubbed his palm on Gallo's bushy black hair. "Also, by then, we may have lots more to talk about flying," concluded Colonel Sami Yusuf.

Chapter 11--Life After Work

LIKE MEMBERS OF T.G.I.F. society, Sami and Roman met, in civvies, at the Aviano Restaurant, not far from the base. Colonel Yusuf was clad in blue jeans, topped with a Giants' baseball cap. Airman Gallo wore a T-shirt with a statement: "Hashers Do Not Rehash. They Just Have A Bash!" They took up a table near the window, ordered drinks and the specialty dinner of the house. Today it was fresh bass and clam chowder. True blue Italians could always order spaghetti, ravioli or other pasta.

In the meantime, Sami asked Roman to explain his T-shirt, as promised earlier.

"It's a fun group that passes the time creatively, accompanied by good beer," said Gallo.

"What's creative about killing time," Yusuf smirked.

"For example, one time we played rabbit and hound in a forest," Roman sipped his Chianti. "I was picked as the rabbit. I took off ahead of the pack, carrying a bag of flour, dropped clues at various stops, by leaving spots of flour here and there, trying to mislead them. Whoever found me first got a prize, Roman beamed, as Sami yawned. "I got bored too when they first described it to me. Taking part in it, turned out to be so much fun." The airman made room at the table for the arriving fish dinner.

Right then, walked in a tall service man with a thick moustache, Groucho-Marx eye brows and a bald patch on his head. Gallo could not miss who that was. He waived him over and introduced him to Colonel Yusuf. "Meet my good friend Adrian Bates," said Roman. "Please join us," he added.

"It's bass night; can't miss it," declared Adrian joyously. "I prefer my own bass, but this will do," he grinned.

"Oh, by the way, Colonel, Master Sergeant Bates is also a Bass Buster!" said Airman Gallo.

"Anyone can become one. Just join our American-Paisano Bass Club," said Adrian; "we fish in the Adriatic, named after me." They all laughed. " We also have contests with prizes for catcher of the biggest bass," the master sergeant stuck his open palms out, as though measuring a large fish.

"I've heard of those fish tales, and I don't mean fins; how big are they in the Adriatic?" Sami wondered. Adrian figured the average bass there weighed about a pound and a half--smaller than in America, due to over-fishing off the Italian coast. They would not even throw small fish back into the water, as done in the US. It was all too fishy for landlubber Sami. By now, Adrian's plate arrived. He placed his fork flat and gently pressed down on the bass.

"Fairly tender. I'd say it's this morning's catch," said the master sergeant, putting on the air of an expert fisherman. Colonel Yusuf asked if he had won any contests. Bates hesitated then said: "Well, a couple," and quickly changed the subject.

Just then a young man in lederhosen, wearing a yodeler's hat marched into the restaurant. Sami seemed to recognize him, but could not recall which October Fest bar in Germany. Then it hit him.

"I'll be damned if that's not Brain!" Colonel Yusuf guffawed, rose and invited him over.

"What have you got to say for yourself, Staff Sergeant Brainerd Gaynor," Roman and Sami said almost in unison. Adrian paused a second, from his delicious bass, to say hello. The blue-eyed Nordic blond blushed a little, and sat in the fourth chair. "Good choice of hairpiece," added Sami.

"You guys invaded my little secret hideaway," smiled Gaynor. "Now I'll have to go back to my tuxedo!" Brain picked up the menu and ordered quiche.

"Manly lederhosen don't go with quiche," said Sami with a slight furtive wink. The colonel cleared his plate then asked if Brain or Adrian had visited Rome recently.

"No, can't fish there," said Bates. But Gaynor was there about a month before.

"Did the Pope bless you," Roman raised his wine glass.

"If he knew the night spots I'd been to, he would give up on me," Brain chuckled. Sami wished to visit Rome, but only to see the Pope come out into the papal balcony to bless the crowds. Roman told him, that those occasions were rare indeed. He recommended Venice, unless he wanted to coincide his visit with the doge's appearance in his balcony.

"I thought there are no longer any doges in Venice," Sami looked puzzled.

"Exactly, so you can go there any time!" Gallo drew on his ribbing humor. Yusuf smirked, but still wanted to know what occasions would the Pope appear on the balcony. "I'd say on Christmas Day, Easter Sunday, and a couple other holy occasions," Roman continued. "If you really want to see him close, he is carried in his Popemobile when conducting service in the main Rome Cathedral," added Gallo.

"What's he doing leaving his Vatican country, traveling to Italy without a visa," Sami grinned sarcastically.

"He is the Bishop of Rome, you know," said Airman Gallo.

Bates finished his fish, then excused himself, to go to a club meeting. Gallo expected a long distance call from his wife in Rome, and left for his abode. Sami and Brain, having more in common, relaxed and let it all hang out emotionally between the two of them.

"Now you can tell me exactly where in Rome you visited, that triggered your excommunication by the Pope," Sami looked into Gaynor's beautiful eyes.

"I went to a drag show. They all sang in Italian, but who cares. The queens were gorgeous." Brainerd straightened his hat. Sami asked if they both could visit Rome when their off-days ever matched.

"Hell, we can match them. I have some pull with the paper shufflers." Brain gave Sami a loving look.

"How about next month? I'll have got essential crap out of the way." Sami watched the waiter drop the plate with the bill on the table. "Do you have a lover who might get jealous?" added Sami.

"A semi-lover in Rome. He is a drag queen, and too busy to be jealous," smiled Brainerd; "what about you, Sami?"

"You mean Luke. We're rainy-day lovers. Always there for each other in tough times," Sami was wistful.

"It's a deal then," said Brain, as Sami placed the money in the plate. "My treat, Brain, since you'll be a free tour guide for me in Rome," concluded Sami.

They strolled leisurely towards the base, taking short side trips through Town Square, Gray Mall and the Aviano soccer stadium, which was eerily silent. Brain lead Sami across the parking lot, into a dark private corner. They held hands, and behind some shrubbery the two kissed passionately.

"They don't ask, we don't tell," said Sami, as the two suppressed a guffaw.

Chapter 12--A Christmas Train Trip

COLONEL SAMI YUSUF AND Staff Sergeant Brainerd Gaynor managed to get their Christmas leaves to coincide. The plan was to see the best of Italy by train, starting with Venice. But first how to get from Aviano to the Venice line. There was no direct rail service to the city of canals. The nearest station en route to Venice, had to have a good schedule of trains.That was Sacile, about half hour drive. A local train did run from Aviano to Sacile, but they had been cautioned that the station was in a bad part of town.

Airman Roman Gallo had very much wanted to spend Christmas in Rome, with his wife and her folks. He was outmaneuvered by rank, and the necessity to stagger some leaves. By the time he learned of Sami and Brain's trip to Rome, Gallo's anger had faded. He offered them a ride to Sacile's rail station. In return, he asked if they could take some gifts to his wife and her mother. The packages were small--a gold necklace for the spouse and perfume for her mom. Sami and Brain thought it was a fair trade.

On this sunny and cold December, Roman picked up Sami Yusuf and Brainerd. On the way to the Sacile rail link, they passed by a house with pink trim.

"There goes a gay house," Sami pointed in jest.

"You're not kidding," said Brain, "That's the popular house of Miss Sheehy--spelled S-H-E/H-E; got it?" he grinned..

"Quite a character around town," added Roman, as they arrived at the Sacile station. Brain and Sami waved farewell to Roman, and wished him a happy Italian Christmas.

"I prefer your Roman one; have a good holiday anyway," Gallo waved back.

In Venice, they got off at the Grand Canal, with Brain humping a backpack of trip essentials, and Sami pulling a Pierre Cardin suitcase on casters. Brain dumped his load onto Sami's rolling luggage, till they checked into a tourist hotel.

The two American Air Force men, dressed in jeans, went on to explore this historic city of canals. They had heard so much about it. On the Bridge of Sighs, Sami looked into Brainerd's eyes and sighed himself; both smiled. On the canal, below, an elderly couple, still in love, intoned that Dean Martin classic of their heyday "Arrivederci Roma", with the serenading Italian gondola oarsman. Sami and Brain could not resist the temptation. They walked over to the rental place, and soon floated down the canal in a smaller less expensive gondola. There was joy on their faces, and twinkle in their eyes, as they surveyed the little paradise around them. Their eyes would meet every now and then. This Venetian whirl was a world away from Aviano and don't-ask-don't-tell Uncle Sam.

Suddenly, Sami went quiet and gloomy.

"What's wrong, Sami?" Brainerd held his hand.

"When I left Baghdad for America, I promised Dad I'd show him Venice in a boat, while I sing for him Abdul Wahab's Gondola song. I can never do it," Sami looked down.

"Why on earth not, Sami?" Brainerd put his arm around Sami's waste.

"Because of a son-of-a-bitch in Rome. Some day I'll tell you about it," Sami feigned a smile, as the gondola returned to its mooring. They jumped out.

"Don't blame others for your bad singing voice," Brain tried hard to get a laugh out of him. Failing that, he dragged Sami to the Basilica Di San Marco, an architectural wonder to Brain. For Sami, it was a reminder of the great golden domed mosque of Baghdad, not far from his dad's residence. Brainerd then lead Sami to see the Palazzo Ducale. The Doge's Palace was hovering like a mirage above the lagoon. Sami's thoughts flew back to when his father took him to visit a family friend at the Great Mesopotamian Marshes. Brain could not understand how that could compare with this seemingly floating mansion. Sami had to recall some Iraqi geography for Brainerd.

"At their height, when dad and I visited there, it was a huge watery substrate, extending over nearly eight thousand square miles. It was home and food source for two hundred thousand Marsh Arabs, known locally as Ma'adan," said Sami.

"You're joshin'," Brain eyed Sami, expecting a burst of leg-pulling laughter. None came forth. "How could so many people live in marshes?" he added.

"Well, they lived in houses made from reeds on small islands, formed where the rivers Tigris and Euphrates meet," said Sami. "Dad said: see these folks; they own very few worldly things, but possess much honor. Without honor, a man is nothing." Sami yearned to see his father again. "This doge fella sure owned a lot of brick. I wonder how much honor he had to go with it," Sami smiled, seeming to snap out of a mini depression. Brain sighed in relief.

The following morning they hopped on a train to Bologna. Across the aisle sat a lady, staring at Brain. She seemed too elegantly dressed for this train. Sign of man in drag, he concluded. He tried not to meet her eye. Presently, a plump female showed up and claimed the lady's seat. The two argued with gestures for five minutes, then the heavyset woman left, looking disgusted. Watching all this, it occurred to Brain that the overdressed gal was familiar.

"I'll be a two-humped camel, if that's not Sheehy," Brain whispered to Sami, as the lady moved over to their side.

"Americanos? " she peered in their faces. Sami and Brain nodded; "Aviano? No?" she pushed back her wig.

"Aviano, yes," Brain replied in a prankish manner. He introduced Sami and himself formally, even though he'd seen her, and heard her being the butt of jokes by Air Force prudes. She presented herself as Toni. Or could have been Tony, Brain thought. "We passed by your house on the way," said Brainerd. She was astounded that airmen knew so much about her, even though she was the only unabashed transvestite for miles around Aviano. Brain and Toni hit it off, then immersed into conversation. Sami reverted back to his favorite book: The Encyclopedia of Scandals. Suddenly Toni noticed a picture in Sami's book.

"That's Ambrosi, I met him in Garbo. He famous?" she beamed.

"Yes, as Pio Faggini, the Pope's butler. You date in the Vatican?!" Sami glanced skeptically at Toni. "What's Garbo?" Sami turned to Brain.

"Oh that; um... a famous gay bar in Rome," said Brainerd eyeing the book's title. "What does it say about him?"

"It says here his head was bashed in with a brass candelabra in his Rome apartment," Sami raised his head and looked at Toni.

"Il Papa or no, he look just like Ambrosi," Toni stared at the photo.

"Where does it say he was gay?" Brain' eyes searched the page. "Here it is: 'a homosexual porno-graphic movie was found in his VCR'. So there you are!" read Brainerd, flitting his eyes between Toni and Sami. "If I was the Pope's waiter, I'd use a different name too, wouldn't you?" Brain looked at both.

"I'd say the Pope as well as his servant, are a disgrace to their religion," said Sami, with Toni and Brain offering a puzzled look. "They both lead double lives. The butler paid for it. The Pope hasn't yet," added Sami pensively.

"Poor Ambrosi. Very nice man. He invite me to his apartment, but I no go; too old. No oomph; capisce? you understand?" said Toni. Brain and Sami nodded without clarifications, despite the heavy Italian accent.

The train pulled into the Bologna station. Toni saw her lover waving at the platform and split. Sami and Brain checked their luggage in the station, pending a later train to Florence. Meanwhile, they had a late lunch at a restaurant, famous for its stuffed pastas, pork cuisine and grated cheese. The part-time Italian waiter was a language student at Bologna University. He was anxious to practice his English on tourists. While taking orders, he asked if any of the two knew that Paris and Bologna were the cultural capitals of Medieval Europe; that the university was a thousand years old.

"We're not hungry for knowledge, just for food," said Sami; "they told me Bologna has great lasagna. Get me that, " he ordered. Brainerd wanted to try the same dish. The waiter left with the orders, his English exercise on hold for now.

The trip to Florence was uneventful, as Sami dozed off, reading the scandal book. It slipped and fell on the floor. Brain picked it up and gingerly placed it beside Sami, so as not to wake him. He then himself caught a little nap, until he heard city sounds. He woke up with the sun low in the horizon, and the Arno River in view. Firenze signs were showing up, as the train approached Florence's main station. They had only two hours, before the Eurostar fast train would leave for Rome, with them aboard. They left their luggage in a locker for the time being.

Sunset lights lingered on, as Brainerd urged Sami to follow him towards the Ponte Vecchio, across the Arno River. The bridge came into view as the sun was setting, while the river shimmered in the red light. It was a sight Sami would recall whenever Florence, or the Tuscany region would be mentioned. With the sun almost gone, Brain lead a brisk walking rundown on Florentine art in the fifteenth century, the Golden Age of Florence, during the reign of Lorenzo de Medici. Even Michelangelo was there, before leaving for Rome. But Sami just wanted to see Donatello's naked statue of David, wearing the hat. With the train leaving for Rome in an hour or so, that's all they had time for anyway. Brain had seen the statue before. He still got excited all over again, as the two went around it half a dozen times. Soon they realized that they had to rush back to the train station. They got there, as the sleek Eurostar train was arriving. The front end resembled a giant head of a snake, followed by a hissing, clickety-clacking long body on myriad wheels.

Chapter 13--Destination Rome

SAMI AND BRAIN SAT in the last coach as the sleek, glistening train slowly slid out of Florence's main train station. No one else was in the compartment, so the two relaxed. The train soon reached high speeds, as Frlorence quickly became a memory. Before long, Tuscany followed suit. Brain, looking through the window, was mesmerized by the lights, while Sami was reading a book. It was now mostly dark outside. Brain turned his eyes towards the interior of the compartment, observing Sami doing his little thing.

"Is that a porno book?" Brain had just read the title.

"No, why do you ask?" said Sami.

"What does 'Unzipped' mean to you for a title?" Brain moved closer to read the finer print.

"It's about some popes in Vatican history," said Sami, rising from his laid-back position. He handed the book to Brain, who flipped through it, then read the blurb about the author.

"What do you expect an atheist to write about religion?" said Brainerd.

"Dr. Ide is a well known author and professor. The book is based on actual facts," Sami turned some pages over, "it says here a wealthy Borgia cardinal bought the papacy with twelve million dollars, and took a mistress from an influential family. This ensured his election--to be Pope Alexander VI," Sami's forefinger was moving right along the page. Brainerd spotted a morsel on page thirty five.

"Here's a pope that's one of us," he smiled." It says that Pope St. Gregory brought in young, blond boys from northern Europe and Scandinavia for sex," Brain glanced at Sami then went back to the book. "Now something about the Quran. Isn't that your Islamic holy book?" Brainerd said. Sami nodded. "That same Pope says here, that Heaven was filled, not as the Quran says, with dark-eyed maidens, but lovely boys. What's wrong with that, Sami?" Brain laughed. Sami was not amused at the papal corruption, nor at the desecration of the Islamic holy book. It had always been so revered by his dad.

"I don't know why a bad pope, such as this new one, should not be treated like any other worthless human being, as was done to Pope St. Hadrian III." Sami flipped to page sixty. "This ninth century pope, enjoyed watching noble women getting whipped, while being forced to walk naked, through the streets," said Sami.

"He was a saint for a reason," Brain smirked.

"Maybe because he was savagely murdered in a bloody vendetta. I don't blame the folks who did it one tiny bit." Sami raised a clenched fist. Brain held Sami's hand and gazed in his face.

"You know, Sami, we've bonded during this trip, and I care about you. I don't give a rat's ass about popes," Brain moved closer; "why do popes, especially this one, bother you so much?" Brain said.

"You're asking for a family secret, that's buried so deep in my psyche. I'm not sure your rope and bucket can retrieve it, out of the depths of my mind's well," Sami grew pensive. Brain pleaded with him to at least try.

With a sympathetic ear facing him, he poured out all that was bottled up. He started with the newly elected Pope molesting him, when he was still Father Rogan, teaching Sami at Baghdad Jesuit High, all these many years ago. The worst of it, was being sodomized at fourteen, by his mentor then, now pope. In Iraqi culture, family honor had been soiled, and must be cleansed by the death. That would either of Sami, by his folks, or the perpetrator by Sami. He could then face his dad again, and visit the family.

"Well then, it's settled. You can't kill the Pope, and your folks can't kill you, if you don't go to Iraq. Why not stay here and enjoy the civilized West?" Brainerd tried to cheer Sami.

The Eurostar train, with the smooth, shiny front engine coach, slowed from its super speed, down to a crawl. It came to a clean stop, at Roma Termini, Rome's main station. Brainerd wasn't sure Regina could make it from the club. It was almost midnight, drag-show time. Sami was following Brain's eyes, being the experienced Rome connoisseur, he presumed. Brain's face lit up, when he caught sight of a drag queen, on high heels, and holding an American flag, stumble towards the train. Brain picked up his backpack and rushed out, with Sami wheeling his bag, in tow. Regina hugged Brain, like he had just been rescued from an enemy POW camp, repeating "Membroso", her pet name for Brainerd. At the first pause, Brain introduced her to Sami. She politely shook his hand, with a jealous look in her eyes. Sami wasn't sure how to greet this fiery Italian quasi woman, in mink coat, high heels, and a dangling stole that matched the coat.

"I didn't think you could make it on a Friday night," said Brainerd.

"Told Gino must do my show early, Membroso coming tonight," Regina pushed back her wig. Brain put his arm above her mink stole, squeezed a little, pulling her head to touch his, and all three marched out of the station. Sami thought 'Membroso' was a cute moniker, and wanted to call him that too. Brain chuckled, then warned Sami that he would be strangled if he dared call him 'Membroso' in Italy or in the company of Italians, anywhere on planet Earth! When asked why not, Brain whispered in Sami's ear, that it was like calling him Big Dick, in America. Whereupon Sami quickly replied, that he learned something new every day.

"What's with this American flag? Is there a war I don't know about?" Brain laughed at Regina, as Sami smiled politely.

"When dress like this, vaffanulo d'un polizia no ask questions, when I in hurry," Regina said exuberantly, like she was proud of her clever idea.

"Did it work with the fuckin' police?" Brainerd looked at her flag.

"With polizia good. With Americanos no. They want to talk and kiss. But I save for my dear Membroso," Regina hugged Brain tighter. At her Fiat, Brainerd asked whether she could drop them off at Altavilla hotel, if she was going downtown. She was happy to drop Sami off there, on Via Principe Amadeo, then return with Brain to her place on Via San Giovanni. Brainerd would not split from Sami.

"Why? You love him but no love me?" Regina pouted.

"Now, now. Sami is my good friend and a stranger in Rome. I've liked you a lot for much longer time," Brain pulled a Kleenex and wiped a little tear off her cheek.

"Si, si, but you love me?" she looked plaintively.

"Yes, darlin', off course I do," Brain gave her a light kiss on the lips, hoping to placate her.

"Good then, I make room in my apartment for three. Small but enough." She tucked herself behind the steering wheel, as Brainerd gently closed the door on her, and walked over to the front passenger seat. In the meantime, Sami made himself comfortable in the back, not sure how to handle this touchy situation. The three, crowded into her small car, heading for Laterano, near the Colosseum, where Regina had lived as long as Brain had known her.

"Nice name, Regina. What does it mean?" Sami tried to make conversation, on the way.

"Means 'queen'," jumped in Brain, "and a damn good drag queen she is," he said. They all laughed, breaking the ice with Sami, as the newcomer.

Chapter 14--Rex/Regina:
Rome's Drag Queen

COLONEL SAMI YUSUF AND Airman Brainerd Gaynor would rise and shine, reveille style, early next morning. Military habits died hard, even when they were on leave, in Rome. From the apartment window, Sami got excited over the partial view of the distant Colosseum. Its sun-splashed walls were sharp and clear, but the shadows totally hid the rest. Seeing it for the first time, Sami recalled the grandeur of ancient Rome, as well as Nero's upside-down crucifixion of the first pope, St. Peter. Sami hated the pedophile popes that followed.

Sometime later, a young man, sporting a crew cut for hair, wearing red pajamas, and Versace sun glasses, popped into the living room.

"Bon giorno," he smiled broadly. Brain greeted her with a broad grin. Seeing Sami a little flustered, Brainerd introduced the young gentleman.

"Sami, meet Rex, the King of Italy during the day, and Queen of Rome at night," said Gaynor. "You already met Queen Regina last night," Brain added. Sami relaxed, rose and hugged Rex.

"Short live the King, but long live the Queen!" proclaimed Sami, kissing him on the cheek. By now he felt accepted and part of the mini-family. Rex then made a hand-to-mouth gesture to both.

"Mangia, mangia?" he said. Brain pointed to his empty stomach, and nodded vigorously. Rex walked to the kitchen and started the clang of dishes, kettle and cutlery.

"You gonna have frittata for breakfast," said Brain to Sami.

"Sounds great, what is it?" Sami stretched his neck towards the kitchen, but could not make out anything, behind the pots and wine rack.

"Omelet, Italian style--fluffy and unfolded," Brainerd chuckled.

Rex proudly walked in, with his frittata and espresso, pulled up a chair and joined his two guests. He then downed a pill, before taking a gulp of the coffee. Rex noticed Sami's puzzled eyes, staring at him.

"Not high blood," he pointed up, "make big chest for Regina," said Rex.

"Oh, female hormones. What do you call it?" Brain looked at Sami.

"Must be estrogen," said Sami, who also wondered how the strict Catholic Church looked at this.

"Ambrosi like it very much. He come see Regina in Tre V every Sabato," Rex was waving triple fingers, then kissed their tips. Sami wondered what was Tre V and who Ambrosi was. Rex tried to explain that it was Rex's gay nightclub, the 3V's for 'Veni Vidi Vici'; that Ambrosi was the Pope's gentleman-in-waiting, as Brainerd put it, helping Rex along with the English.

"You mean butler?" Sami sliced another piece of frittata.

"No, no; Ambrosi take big people to see Il Papa," Rex rattled in his Italian English.

"He escorts famous guests to the papal apartments, and chats with them until the Pope is ready for the interview," Brain explained for Sami. He glanced at Rex, who nodded in agreement.

"I don't get it. The Vatican hates homosexuals, but Big Chief has a gay secretary, who goes to a gay bar with a funny name," Sami frowned. "Then again, if they make a pope out of a child molester, like Rogan, nothing should surprise me," Sami half mumbled to himself, but unintelligibly to Rex. It was clear enough to Brainerd, who sat pensively, sipping his coffee.

"Veni-Vidi-Vici not funny name. Julius Caesar said it when he fight in Turkey," said Rex. "In Latin, mean I came, I saw, I conquered".

Sami rose, walked to his suitcase, rummaged through it. He came back with a beautifully decorated sheath and a handle. Slowly, he pulled out a shiny golden dagger. It sparkled in Rome's night light, that beamed through the windows, and lit up the apartment.

"Poppone! Bello oro!" Rex stared in awe at the dazzling gold surface. Sami handed it to Rex, who held it with his two hands, ever so carefully. "Why you bring this with you. Gold must be in box, in banca," said Rex.

"It's a family heirloom from my great grandfather. I brought it as a gift for the Pope," said Sami, with a stone face. Brainerd moved closer, ostensibly to admire the dagger. He felt its edges.

"Sharp as a ginsu knife! What are you up to, Sami?" whispered Brainerd, when Rex was distracted for a minute. He then rejoined the two, who quickly went silent.

"Why give to our Papa. You are Muslim--give to your big Ayatollah," Rex smiled admiringly.

"He was my teacher at the Jesuit high school in Baghdad," said Sami sheepishly.

"Padre Eterno! He is joking, no?" Rex eyed Brain, who nodded. "I tell Ambrosi to talk to Il Papa," said Rex.

"No, no; it should stay in the family," Brain interjected, with a deathly look of concern.

"Let's forget about it now, and go see Roma, yes?" Rex buttoned up his jean jacket and pulled up the pants zipper. They all concurred, then piled into Rex's Fiat, and onto the Colosseum for a first stop. The Vatican was Sami's primary interest. They moved on there, after that.

Chapter 15--Reconnoitering the Vatican

ST. PETER'S SQUARE WAS so much bigger than it looked on Luke's TV, in San Francisco. That is when Heinrich Dengler, the head Cardinal, declared 'Habemus Papam', upon presenting Cardinal Rogan to the world, as the new Pope Urban IX. It grated on Sami's nerves, no end. Right now, only a few tourists were walking around in the immense space. It was a far cry from the tens of thousands that jammed the square, when Dengler introduced the new Pope, in Latin. Sami wanted to know exactly where the Pope appeared. Rex pointed to the basilica's central balcony, overlooking St. Peter's Square.

"If you like blessing from Il Papa, come Christmas or Easter. He bless you and everyone in big piazza," said Rex. Sami eyed the distance from the papal balcony to Rome's buildings, outside the Vatican borders, which faced that balcony.

"Would be nice if I could watch the Pope from the veranda of an opposite hotel," said Sami.

"Isn't it easier just to watch from the Square? All around is Vatican, except the wide Via delle Conciliazione, going straight out, as far as you can see. That leaves you some rooftops," Brain's forehead creased up. "What are you up to, Sami?" he quickly added. "Mehmet Ali Agca tried it on John Paul II, at close range, without a telescoping rifle, and did not miss. They both lived to be very old men. Agca, now in a Turkish jail, still has his date with the Pope's boss," Brainerd rolled his eyes skyward. Sami looked down and went silent. "Let's go have fun, Sami. It's time to forget ancient hurts." Brain held Sami's hand and dragged him towards the Egyptian obelisk. It stood like a lonely branchless tree, landscaping the center of St. Peter's Square. It pained Sami to witness this priceless piece of ancient Arab-land history which was plundered out of its original home, inside Egypt's Temple of the Sun, at Heliopolis. Emperor Caligula had shipped it to Rome in 37 AD. It took Pope Sixtus, in 1585, to drag this column of Pharoah Amenemhet, and plant it in the Vatican square, where it now towered over an awe-inspired Sami.

"You're telling me I can never see my dad again," said Sami, tears streaming down his cheeks.

"If you must do it your way, babe, you definitely will not see your folks again," said Brainerd, squeezing Sami's hand. Rex, not privy to their inner thoughts, asked why Sami was unhappy. Brain interjected that the beauty of Rome brought tears to Sami's eyes.

"Ah, wait for Club Tre V. We make you laugh till mattino," said Rex.

"That's right, till dawn," Brain echoed. At the obelisk, Sami perked up. He felt a kinship with anything Egyptian, an Arab country like Iraq. However, he wished that European countries had not looted the treasures of ancient Egypt. It definitely included this Vatican one. The Ramses square obelisk was taken from Thebes and stuck in a round hole, at the Place de la Concorde, in Paris. Rex assured him that Rome's obelisk was saved from destruction, being protected in the Eternal City, all these centuries. To give Sami a little feel of home, they took him to the Egyptian Museum inside the Vatican. Sami went into a reverie, gazing at the Iraqi bas-reliefs from the palaces of King Sargon II and Sennacherib, brought from Nineveh.

"Ambrosi invite me here, after he saw my show at 3V, first time, " said Rex; "he says these are quasi, how you say, almost three thousand old."

"I feel I have been that many years away from Baghdad," Sami snapped back to attention. Brainerd wanted to see the Sistine Chapel next, but Sami resisted. He recalled the election of the hated Rogan to be the new Pope. The lure of Michelangelo and Botticelli proved too much, and Sami joined Brain and Rex. He stood in awe at the master's famous frescoes, entirely covering the barrel-vaulted Sistine ceiling. Seeing the dates painted--1508 to 1512, then 1534 to 1541--Sami wondered what kind of paint would last all these centuries.

"I'd be very happy if my Aaron Brothers paints lasted ten years," Sami laughed. Brainerd was glad to see him quit his sad state of mind. Rex thought it was a good time for a break at the bar.

"Where would you find a bar at this Basilica?" said Sami.

"There, alla cima--top, top!" said Rex pointing to the roof of St. Peter's; "cafe too--mangia mangia".

It was an astounding revelation to Sami, still used to the dry Islamic religion. He thought it was too high a climb for a little break. Rex assured him that elevators carried tourists to the dome of this structure, built centuries before elevators were invented. They went for a snack first, in the Cafeteria. Later at the bar, Rex had a Chianti. Brain went for a White Russian, with that vanilla ice cream and vodka, which suited his personality. Sami settled for a latte. After a while, Rex suggested a better view from the Lantern, atop the dome. They were rested enough to climb the stairway, between the inner and outer casing of the dome, leading to the external gallery of the Lantern. Sami was amazed by the view, looking down at the gardens of the Vatican Palace. People, the size of dwarfs were seen moving about. Beyond the great Square, the panorama engulfed the Eternal City. Sami was looking for recognizable hotels with a reverse view to the Vatican. When eyed by Brain, Sami looked away into a different direction.

Leaving the Vatican and St. Peter's Square, Rex waved at a Swiss guard, whom he'd seen with Ambrosi.

"That one served with Hans, who killed Colonel Braun, over there, few years before," said Rex pointing to an apartment just beyond the guards' barracks, near the main entrance to St. Peter's Square. There was a sudden pause in Sami's gum chewing, wanting to know how and why it happened. Rex recalled the events, as best as he could. The Pope had appointed Braun as the new commandant of the Swiss Guards. Before the papal swearing-in ceremony, Hans went to Colonel Braun's Vatican apartment and shot both him and his wife, then killed himself. Sami kept asking why. It turned out that Braun had reprimanded Hans, who had bottled up his anger, until he exploded into the killing binge.

Before heading home, Rex figured his visitors might want to see another papal structure: Rome's Basilica of St. John Lateran, which was the Pope's church, as the Bishop of Rome.

"He kiss stinky feet of old priests here," said Rex. He held his nose, as they passed by the church. Sami laughed, wondering if the Pope was also a foot fetishist, besides being a molester.

"Now that's nasty," Brain pressed Sami's nose. "This is how the Pope commemorates the Last Supper, when Jesus kissed the feet of the apostles, as a sign of humility." Brain got an apology from Sami. He added that the Muslims considered Christ as their prophet too. But this pope was a different animal.

"Christians like Pat Roberson would rather commit hara-kiri, than say a good word about Prophet Muhammad," Sami smirked.

Chapter 16--A Gay Roman Evening

BY EIGHT IN THE evening, Rex, Brain and Sami made it to the nightclub. The big sign above the entrance read "TreV", for the three V's that summarized the lower line "Veni Vidi Vici" in Julius Caesar's famous battle dispatch from Turkey, meaning: "I came, I saw, I conquered". The club borrowed it as a sneaky promotional stunt. It suggested that those who would 'come' to the nightclub would 'see' their darling guy, then 'conquer' and take him home. A heavy, bulging suitcase was weighing Rex down, as Brain helped at the handle. Everyone seemed to know Rex, and made way for him and his baggage-aiding entourage. He greeted acquaintances with "buona notte", good night, and friends with"ciao", hello. A short guy propositioned Rex, who waved him off with "no, membrolino", to the delight of others.

"He called him 'small dick'," whispered Brain to Sami. He suppressed an explosive reaction.

Reaching the stage, Rex hopped onto it, humping the suitcase, while Brainerd and Sami stayed to watch with the crowd. Behind the curtains, Rex took some articles out of the suitcase and put them in a small bag, then pushed the suitcase out of sight. Suddenly music played and the curtains went up on a massage parlor scene. There were a couple of adjacent couches, and two restroom doors. One had the 'Finocchio' sign, for faggot, and the other 'Finocchia', for dyke. In the burst of laughter, Rex walked into the women's room, later came out in a gorgeous red gown, with matching red high heels. They shouted "bravo Regina". She then walked into the men's room, and soon came out to a tango tune, dancing cheek-to-cheek with Mussolini. The audience was delighted. After a hilarious performance, she told Mussolini to go sit down like a good Italian. She sensually stripped to Egyptian belly-dancing music. Sami joined in the Arabic tempo, clapping vigorously. She was down to a large fig leaf over the bulging vagina location. Regina then lay, tummy down, on one of the couches, and shouted: "massaggio!".

Mussolini promptly jumped on top of Regina, and feigned intercourse movements. The crowd booed the fascist sex maniac. From the men's room popped out Hitler, wiggling urine drops off his little dick. Looking arrogant as ever, Hitler was still a prick, to the audience. Seeing the couch scene, he undressed, then jumped on top of Mussolini, who was still on top of Regina. Quickly, Regina slipped out from under both of them, and rattled a lot of words. They were gibberish to Sami. Everyone else roared with laughter. She then sat on the other couch, as the lights dimmed.

"Regina told Hitler to go ahead and screw Mussolini instead of Italy." Brain did his best to translate Regina's fast Italian for Sami.

Suddenly the pope, in full regalia, walked in, looking for his butler. He was accompanied by a cute Swiss guard. His holiness blessed everything that moved, as precious life, starting with the two screwing dictators. He then sat next to Regina, with the coat loosely covering her naked body, leaving room for the fig leaf. The pope's servant showed up with the new commander of the Swiss guards, both in jockstrap. The pope pointed a finger at them, as his companion Swiss guard shot in that direction. The commander fell dead, and the butler dragged him offstage.

Desperate to confess her sins, Regina lit up a cigar, shaped like a dildo, and took a deep puff, as the pope listened intently. He told his holiness one sordid incident after another, until the pope fainted. Presently, Saddam Hussein marched in, carrying the Iraqi flag, with the Arabic words on it, translating to "Allah is greater", meaning greater than anybody else on Earth. He noticed the pope lying unconscious, and got him to sniff gunpowder. The pope came to, and started blessing Saddam. He misunderstood the holy hand gestures, and gave the pope the finger. Sami hated Saddam, but thoroughly approved of the symbolic finger put-down, like it was done on his behalf. Hussein moved on, with the Allah-worded flag fluttering, and the pope waving his big cross, as the curtain fell. Regina came out from behind the stage, while Brainerd and Sami were still applauding.

"So glad you like. We arranged Saddam too quick, after Brain tells me today," Regina was being apologetic to Sami.

"How do you say it, perfecto, Regina. I always wanted the new pope fingered, for being a bad man!" said Sami, and hugged Regina. Brain expressed relief that his last-minute idea did not bomb. The show went on with dancing and stripping to sensual music, till the wee hours of the morning.

On the way home, Regina told them if they wanted a real pope act, to be in St. Peter's Square on Easter Sunday, in the morning, for the start of the show, called "Urbi et Orbi".

"What the hell does that mean?" Sami perked up.

"To the City and the World," Brain translated the Latin on behalf of Regina, who could only rattle in Italian. Sami remained puzzled as to the difference between the two languages. He added that he would definitely be there for the papal event. Brain thought Sami was joking. Why would anyone who hated the pope, travel from way north of Italy, just to hear him talk in Latin about Jesus?

Chapter 17--The Plot

THE TRAIN TRIP BACK to Aviano air base lacked Rome's excitement. It was full of nostalgia though, for the fun times, which Sami and Brain had just experienced, with Regina. One fact kept reverberating in Sami's head: "ten thirty, Easter Sunday morning!"

At the base, Sami continued with small-altitude routines, as he trained new pilots in his skilled techniques. Some of the flyers were bound for missions over the mountains of northern Iraq. Others were destined for the flatlands and desert landscapes of central and southern Iraq. Sami wished he was training them inside the motherland of Iraq. But that meant seeing his dad in Baghdad, while still feeling personal shame and family dishonor. This went way back to when his Jesuit teacher, Father Rogan, had violated his trust and youthful body, in the anus. This act alone made it a deathly unforgivable deed. He could only face his folks, after he had cleansed their honor. In Iraqi parlance, that meant full payment by the perpetrator--with his life, and nothing less.

The outlandish nature of the task soon dawned on him. To get to a to well-guarded pope, who was holed up in the labyrinth of the Vatican was well nigh impossible. Sami pushed the idea into his subconscious, as near wishful thinking. Nevertheless, he was determined to honorably see his sick father, before it was too late.

This January and February, the weather in the Dolomite Alps of northern Italy was often unstable. Hence, there were long gaps of inactivity, intermingled with abbreviated periods of flight training. Lost time was made up by enhanced scheduling in March and early April, including Easter Sunday. Though not Christian, Sami always relaxed on Easter Sunday anyway, especially when he was with Luke in San Francisco. To work on that day, was a great disappointment for him.

Then, in a diabolical brainstorm he came to the conclusion. He had one fleeting opportunity to restore his honor. That was when Pope Urban IX would appear on the balcony, to bless the crowds in St. Peter's Square, on Easter Sunday. Sami called the local catholic church, and found out that the Pope would show up in the papal balcony, at exactly ten in the morning. The responding priest told Sami, how lucky he was to be blessed, in person, by His Holiness. Sami barely contained himself, as he slammed the receiver onto its rest.

Reality then dawned on Sami. If he carried out his plan, how would he escape, and where to? How far could he fly? What maximum distance could he extend the plane's range? The safest route that would take him to Baba, his dad. His Baghdad neighborhood was now free of the tyrant's terror, but was in pro-American control. That, notwithstanding, as a Sunni, how could he cross Shiite neighborhoods to get to Baba? Then he recalled his father's advice: with a complicated project, concentrate on one step at a time, to preserve your sanity!

Sami blocked out everything from his mind, except the papal balcony, overlooking St. Peter's Square, on Easter Sunday, at 10 a.m.

He pulled out his topographic map of Italy--the one he had been using for near-ground flights. Marking the exact distance from Aviano to the Vatican, Sami calculated the precise velocity of the plane, weighted down by two heavy missiles. Despite colonel Yusuf's murderous thoughts, he dutifully dropped by General Amal with an idea. He would be willing to make up for lost winter time, by flying early on Easter Sunday, with a real-time fully loaded jet, for battle-ready rehearsal. Impressed by his officer's conscientious initiative, the general gave him the go-ahead signal.

Aviano was in languor, as Good Friday arrived. The sky was calm and clear, except for a few cloud puffs. Colonel Yusuf gave the order to fully fuel the newest F-16 fighter jet, and fit it with two sidewinder missiles. It must be battle-ready for low-flight training, the next day, Saturday. It was the eve of Easter Sunday. Sami got easy approval from the Base Commander, to make up for lost winter time. Admiring Sami's diligence, the men went to work, getting the plane ready, that same day--Friday. This was in case the colonel decided to train early Saturday, giving him the option of taking Easter Sunday off. Little did they know. Not even a slight hint ever leaked out from Sami, as to what they were helping him do.

Sunday morning finally arrived. The blue sky was dotted with small clouds of various shapes. It was more suitable for a painter with an easel, than a pilot on a deadly mission. The extended weather forecast did not indicate rain, nor disruptive weather. Colonel Sami Yusuf took a deep breath, stared at his dad's photo on the wall, and jumped out of bed. He washed and shaved closely, like he expected no more than a short stubble, when his personal mission was over. He drank a can of Ensure for a quick breakfast, suited up, and donned his helmet, then headed for the ready plane. It was too early on this Easter Sunday, for anyone to see Colonel Yusuf off. He was experienced enough to take off without bothering anyone, and it was just fine with Sami, anyway.

The plane lifted, and immediately distanced itself from the buildings, so as not to waken anyone. It quickly rose to ten thousand feet, till Sami was clear of the base and urban vicinity. He then veered in the direction of Rome. Green fields, and undulating hills came into view. He then descended to a lower altitude. All was calm and peaceful beneath him. Even the farmers were off-duty this Sunday, despite lazily-grazing unattended cows, which he could clearly see. They could not care less, and that was OK with Sami.

It was now quarter to ten in the morning of this Easter Sunday. He figured on flying over to the sea, ten miles north of Rome, then veering back in, towards the Vatican. Getting closer to the sea, Sami lost some of his single-minded determination, and got a little fidgety. What if the Pope was late? He could not keep circling around the papal balcony! It would wreck this opportunity of a lifetime to settle the age-old account with his nemesis. On the other hand, if all went well, the Pope should be in sight very soon.

Presently the green fields were gone and it was just the blue sea. Sami turned the plane around towards the Eternal City for a deadly assignment, should God not intervene. The clock's 9:58 a.m. seemed to jump out and dazzle his eyes. Then he saw shouting crowds in a huge square. They were waving at a balcony on the edge of St. Peter's Square. Sami knew that he and the Pope were destined to be on time, for their ten o'clock Easter Sunday appointment.

Chapter 18--The Execution

THE NOISY PLANE APPROACHED the packed giant square, at rooftop level. Many tourists, especially Americans, turned, saw U.S. emblems on the fighter, and continued to wave, thinking it was a salute to the Holy Father. Even the Pope looked up, smiled, raised his hand and waved, in approval. Just then Colonel Sami Yusuf released a sidewinder missile towards the balcony, followed by a second rocket, aimed a little higher. The first missile demolished the balcony, dropping debris along with the Pope and two cardinals, far down to the ground. The second weapon went through the loggia's entrance, onto the floor of St. Peter's Basilica, exploding against priceless artifacts. The plane then zoomed past, flying in an easterly direction.

There was pandemonium everywhere. The outer crowds in the huge square stampeded for the city streets, scrambling to get home, any which-way they could. A man in a wheelchair was knocked over, as he frantically tried to roll out of this endless field of humanity. A nun, with the help of others, flipped the chair back on its wheels, and pushed him out of harms way. Suddenly, Roman cops, in La Polizia uniforms, were everywhere, in and around the Vatican square. They quickly went about to secure the area as a crime scene. Simultaneously, the Swiss Guards helped clear St. Peter's Square of all but essential personnel.

By now half a dozen ambulances were at the site of the shattered papal balcony, way below where it once stood. It had been a highly sturdy platform for the Holy Father to bless the Easter crowds, before the free fall to ground level. Soon one ambulance, with the Pope inside, navigated its way through the remaining clusters of grieving men and women. It then screeched past them to Gemelli Polyclinic hospital, in this Eternal City. At the scene, several doctors were attending to the two cardinals. They had flanked the Pope on the balcony, before the attack. They were now sprawled on the ground with the shattered papal balcony all around them. An elderly physician, with a stethoscope, paused and wiped his face. A Jesuit father asked him if the fallen cardinals would make it. The white-haired doctor shook his head sideways. The Jesuit lowered his head, crossed himself, then walked away, as a tear rolled down his cheek. A few minutes later, someone's hand-held radio declared that Boston's cardinal Francis Joseph Lawton, and polish cardinal Casimir Dolinski had just passed away. The two prelates had moved behind the Pope, when the missile hit the balcony. Statements of sorrow quickly followed, from the US and Polish ambassadors to the Vatican. Just then, the broadcaster interrupted radio programs, to announce the death of Pope Urban IX, in the hospital's intensive care unit.

Animated Romans went unexpectedly quiet. Even noisy city cars stopped sounding their horns. There was an eerie silence, that lasted over an hour. Then camerlengo, the papal chamberlain, Cardinal Lazaro Aznar walked through the hospital corridors, followed by a dozen princes of the Catholic church in red skullcaps, as well as bishops and key Vatican officials. Just past the hospital exit doors, at the main entrance, Aznar halted, as did the entourage, in step. Cameras and reporters converged on the hospital's frontage. It was quiet, except for some TV cameras whirring and newsmen jockeying for strategic positions around Lazaro Aznar. The Cardinal surveyed the jostling, scoop-hungry crowd, in front of him. In a broken voice he proceeded:

"I have sad news for you, all Catholics, and the world at large," said Cardinal Aznar. "A short time ago, at ten minutes after one p.m., to be precise, the Holy Father, Pope Urban IX passed away." The cardinal paused, as a commotion spread through the crowd. A masculine middle-aged man wiped a tear, then an old lady fainted, causing a stir. The papal chamberlain took a deep breath, before resuming. "We now start with a forty-day period of mourning." He wiped his face, glanced at German Cardinal Heinrich Dengler, and continued. "After that, the College of Cardinals will meet in the Sistine Chapel, to elect a new Holy Father," said Aznar, with faint, wistful eyes of a potential new pope, as he momentarily fixed his gaze on the other cardinals. "In the meantime, we shall have to manage with no one on the throne of Saint Peter." He fidgeted a bit. "As to who did this ungodly act, the Dean of the College of Cardinals, Dengler, will take it up with the authorities, be it Italian or other countries. The perpetrators will be brought to justice," concluded the camerlengo. He turned around and headed back into the hospital, to start the proceedings for moving the pope's remains, and commence the arrangements for the funeral ceremonies. Weighing heavily on his mind, was providing security for all those world leaders. They would soon converge onto one single location, to pay homage to the departed pontiff. That location would be a highly prized terrorist target.

Chapter 19--The Escape

COLONEL YUSUF KEPT FLYING in an easterly direction, towards Incerlik in Turkey, where the US operated a military air base. He figured that his American fighter plane would not arouse international suspicion, until he decided where he should land. A thousand thoughts crossed his mind. He mulled over a few potential destinations. Each had its advantages and possible deadly drawbacks. But the ultimate goal was making his way from there to his folks in Baghdad, especially his dad. He was now clean, having restored the family honor, by killing the man who had besmirched it. If the violator was a pope, and it had happened way back, at Baghdad's Jesuit highschool, so be it.

With American personnel in Iraq, hc had to pick a landing spot very carefully. He would then have to negotiate his way from the plane, all the way to his father's house, in the capital. But where to land? That was the billion-dinar question. The dinar used to be worth more than three dollars, when Sami had left Iraq, years before. With Baghdad's wars, followed by international embargoes, the dinar had plunged to less than a penny in value. The fugitive US officer had enough dollars on him, to survive without thousands of cheap dinars bulging his pockets.

Colonel Yusuf ruled out landing in Iran. Their grievances against the US, he figured, were not enough for them to shield him from the Americans. Harboring a wanted Iraqi American, would not conform with Iran's claim to be a good neighbor of the new Iraq, he concluded. Sami knew that there were scarcely any Americans in Kurdistan, especially in the northern-most region of the country. The Kurds were very friendly to the Americans--unlike some Arab Islamic sects, in Baghdad and central Iraq.

Sami remembered his roommate, Farhad, at the Jesuit-school's boarding house. He was a Kurd from the city of Zakho, near the Turkish border. Farhad lived on Souk street, when Sami visited him, a long time ago. Zakho was a town of twenty thousand then, a far cry from the current sprawling city, with many times the population of old times. This and other myriad facts, Colonel Yusuf found out, reading the ubiquitous Iraq news in every newspaper around the world.

Could he find his way through this new metropolis, to Farhad's house? He scratched his head, seeking a quick answer. The plane's range and dwindling fuel demanded instant resolution, and decisive action. But where to land? Farhad had told him world war II stories about British planes using a landing strip outside Zakho. Had the city expanded enough to incorporate that mini-airport for civilian housing? If that was the case, where could he then bring the plane down, to a safe stop?

Sami knew two mountain ranges flanked Zakho. Between these tall mountains, were stretches of flat plains, where he could touch down, with acceptable risk, using his cumulative skills in operating this type of craft. If he could walk away, with no more than a scratch, Uncle Sam could afford the loss of one more F-16 plane, he figured. Colonel Yusuf had read about Baghdad's government, paving good roads in Kurdistan, to subdue the rebellious Kurds. They would be fairly old roads by now.

What was their condition that day? Sami was dying to know. It might just save his life, if he landed on such a road. The Iraqi American colonel, on the run, weighed all his options. They were not too many, and none of them was a cinch. Sami graded his choices like a Dale Carnegie exercise, which he had done in San Francisco eons ago, it seemed.

Colonel Yusuf drew a vertical line on a piece of paper. He labeled one column 'Disadvantages' and the other 'Advantages': of landing near the Iraqi-Turkish border city of Zakho. It was a system for choosing the best option, in an intractable situation, as part of a Dale Carnegie chapter, back when life was easy and secure. At the time, he had struggled to invent a problem so he could create the best solution, for a good grade in his employer-paid course. The first column included: capture, enemy combatant, torture and death. The second column had: Farhad sanctuary, trip to Baghdad, see dad while still alive. He then crossed out each item in the 'Disadvantage' column, as risks worth taking. The AWOL colonel was now strangely relaxed, having made a momentous decision. He would use all his skills to land the F-16 fighter jet near Zakho. This Iraqi border town was a short air-hop from Incerlik's US airbase in Turkey. The prospect of American military, so close to his destination, made him apprehensive, but not enough to change his plans. He had made his Dale-Carnegie decision. Sami went through another exercise: how to make the most out of a bad situation. There were two ways to get to Zakho, figured Sami. One would be to fly low, undetected, over Syria's northern terrain, into Kurdistan, at the extreme-northern part of Iraq, ending in Farhad's city. The other route would take him over Turkey, past Incerlik, to Zakho, a few minutes later. He would pretend to end his flight at Turkey's American base, lulling those personnel into a false sense of a simple finale to Sami's escapades. At Incerlik, he would zoom past, and quickly cross Iraq's border, to land near Zakho. The friendly Kurds, no doubt, would embrace him, and lead his way to downtown Zakho. There, Sami would shake them off, then visit Farhad clandestinely, without jeopardizing his good friend. The Syrian path was too risky, he concluded. By the time he would get to Syria, the Middle East could be alerted to fugitive Sami and the fleeing American jet. Their pilots would be waiting for US Air Force's fugitive plane. Colonel Yusuf opted for the Turkish route. He thought that by the time the Turks and Americans had informed the Kurdish authorities, across the border, he was sure to be safe with his ex-roommate, Farhad, who would never give him away.

Chapter 20--Destination Zakho

WHEN POPE URBAN IX was declared dead, the escaping F-16 was flying low, over international waters of the Mediterranean Sea. Sami listened to the cockpit's scratchy radio, broadcasting his misdeed, as well as the type of US military jet to look for. He laughed at some of the alleged sightings. A Tuscan shepherd saw a jet zoom above tree tops, clearly exhibiting the devil's emblem under its wings. A south Argentine ham radio quoted an Antarctica report of a small American airplane landing amongst terrified penguins. It all meant that no one had yet located Sami, who adhered to a near sea-skimming mode, after leaving Rome and the Italian terrain. Colonel Yusuf was now approaching the Turkish coast-- low enough to see fishermen in boats waving at him. The Bosphorus strait was in sight, and now his path was very clear.

He crossed the southern shore of Turkey, with no incident, as the F-16 continued, now hugging the ground. Nothing on his radio or cockpit receiver gave the slightest hint, that Sami's plane was located, by any country, or international body. Why fly over Incerlik, when no one was aware of his presence, Sami questioned himself. It seemed dumb to alert US airbase personnel, just to fool them. So he just clung to a route south of Incerlik, crossing Iraq's Kurdistan border, east of Zakho.

West of the city was a busy thoroughfare, all the way to Khaboor's customs check-point, the official border crossing between Turkey and Iraq. Long lines of trucks and tankers, on the Turkish side, were waiting to cross into Kurdistan. They would buy cheap gasoline and other products in Iraq, then sell them back in Turkey, for a lucrative profit. Sami was delighted at the sight of all those vehicles. It told him that the border personnel were too busy with commerce, to hunt for a runaway airplane, whose pilot had just killed a Christian crusader. When Pope John Paul II was nearly assassinated by a Turk, Sami read that no one in Turkey or Iraq demonstrated against the crime. This lack of interest in Christian matters was comforting to Sami, who saw an escape route through it all.

Surveying the area for a landing stretch, Colonel Yusuf spotted a well-paved road going from Zakho towards the northern border mountains. A former Baghdad despot had built it to suppress the Kurds, Farhad had told him. In the process, the Butcher of Baghdad, as they called him, had destroyed over four thousand Kurdish villages, forcing them into towns like Zakho. That's how the town grew to over twenty times its previous population. With no villagers, or villages in sight, Sami easily touched down on the remote solidly-paved road, a few miles outside Zakho. How ironic that a tyrant's atrocities would help him escape to Baghdad, Sami mused. It seemed obscene to him that someone's tragedy would come as a blessing, here and now. He thought of Frarhad's relatives and friends, who were slaughtered by Baghdad's ruler. It was during the campaign to subjugate Kurdistan, along with massive ethnic uprooting from oil-rich regions.

The plane passed over a festive crowd on a green grassy field, just outside Zakho. Some of them waved at the aircraft. In the old days they would dive in a ditch, or run for their lives, to escape bombs or mustard gas, hurled at them by the Air Force of the despotic government of Iraq. They had not seen a hostile jet since the statue of their nemesis was toppled in Baghdad by the Americans. He recalled Farhad telling him that the Kurds remained America's best friend in the Middle East, despite US acquiescence to atrocities by prior Baghdad's rulers. Sami had a good feeling that he would be safe in Kurdistan, especially here. The Iraqi American colonel was now a couple hundred feet above the asphalt road, which had a small downward grade into a wide shallow valley. Sami came to a halt without incident. The craft was not visible to the crowd, which he just passed over. They were in a lower, concealed plain.

Colonel Yusuf pulled a small bag by the handle, unzipped it, then yanked the blue jeans, a shirt and some warm clothes. Slipping out of his military clothes, he quickly put on civilian pants, shirt, and grey sweater, topped with a thick overcoat. It was a bright and sunny afternoon, though a little chilly on this April day in northern Iraq, near the Turkish border. At the bottom of the bag was a bundle of twenty dollar bills, which he stuffed into his various pockets. Before leaving the fighter jet, in mufti, he cast one last wistful eye inside the plane and his military career.

"Goodbye friend!" Sami whispered, as though ashamed of abandoning a loyal winged companion. He then jumped out of his faithful aircraft and walked briskly towards the festive crowds.

Chapter 21--Wedding Guest

AS SAMI GOT CLOSER to the crowds, he could hear a drumbeat and the sound of a wind instrument. The music and drumming grew louder, as he approached the site. Then he noticed a large ring of men and women, dancing to Kurdish music. Some were waving colored handkerchiefs, in tune. On one side of the ring, were only women, while the rest of the circle were just men. Each one held the happy waving hand of his or her neighbor, like the links in a circular chain. The women were in bright colorful traditional dresses. Many men wore Kurdish garb, consisting of baggy pants and tight jackets, with cloth wrapped around their heads. This distinctively Kurdish turban headgear came in various colors and designs. Other men were dressed in western style clothing. Some had jeans on. A few even wore ties.

Colonel Yusuf passed by a number of picnicking groups, on his way to the dancing circle. Some greeted him, as though he was a guest. He returned the compliments in his decent Kurdish, with a trace of Baghdadi accent. It was tempered by his years of speaking American English. None of that caused a stir among the celebrants. They were used to local ex-patriots returning from the West, after the terror of Baghdad's rulers was squelched by an American invasion. Sami breathed a deep sigh of relief. He knew then and there that he would make it to Baghdad, and see his sick father again.

A man grabbed Sami's hand and pulled him to the ring, unlocked two dancers' hands, in the hopping circle, and joined the dabka-type of dancing, as done by local custom. Not wanting to be noticed as an outsider, Sami picked up a stray red kerchief from the ground, and started jumping and swaying with the rest of the dancers in the ring. Whenever the drummer got closer, those nearest him hopped more vigorously to the high beat. The spirited movements would slow down, as the drummer moved on, around the ring, followed by the reed player. That was when people could hear themselves talk.

"You looked sad and lost, so I dragged you in here. A wedding is a joyous time for everyone. I'm Sabri, what's your name?" he said.

"I'm Sami. Whose wedding is it?" colonel Yusuf stopped waving the brightly-colored kerchief.

"You're here and you still don't know? Didn't Farhad tell you about Shevan's marriage?" Sabri was more amused than amazed, in the midst of this festive ambience

"I was abroad. He mentioned a surprise, when I got back." Sami pretended he was no stranger here. Shevan was a two-year toddler when Sami left Iraq.

A middle-aged balding man was peering through thick glasses, and limping in Sami's direction. Recognizing Farhad, he uncoupled himself from his neighbors and rushed to hug him.

"My God, Sami, I look for you in the heavens, to invite you to my son's wedding, and I find you here on Earth, and in

Zakho to boot! Your college tricks were fantastic, but this one tops them all!" Farhad kissed Sami on both cheeks, Kurdish fashion.

"What happened to your leg?" Sami wasn't sure whether to rejoice at seeing his school friend, or show concern for his leg.

"A stray bullet from a government soldier. They came in during the subjugation campaign against the Kurds. We were lucky not to end up at Abu Ghraib, or some mass grave," smiled Farhad, grateful for being alive.

Sami, not yet ready to tell his story, pretended that Farhad did guess his new trick accurately, as he lead Sami to the family picnic spot

"Look Amina, we got manna from heaven?" said Farhad to his astonished wife.

"It's been a thousand years, Sami." Amina, looking haggard, started to rise. Sami rushed to hug her and begged her not to get up.

"Come here Shevan, greet Uncle Sami," Farhad beckoned to his puzzled son, who had heard so much about this uncle, which is an honorary title given to any elder friend of the family. Shevan remembered seeing Sami so many years ago, but could not recall what he would look like now. The groom jumped up dutifully and extended his hand to shake, but Sami went past his hand and hugged Shevan like a long-lost child.

"How time flies, Shevan. Last time I saw you, I picked you up from the pram and kissed you goodbye," said Uncle Sami, with nostalgia oozing from his eyes. "Where is your bride?" he asked.

"You've been so long in America; did you forget our customs, Uncle? She stays with the women till the wedding ceremony," said Shevan, with a shy smile. Farhad then interrupted.

"Look Sami, I don't care what arrangements await you in Zakho, you are staying with us. We have a nice guest room, and we just found our guest of honor!" beamed Farhad. Colonel Yusuf pretended that he had ready accommodations, but that he would gladly cancel them, to stay and talk old times with Farhad.

Chapter 22--The Protector

IT WAS DUSK, AND the celebrants gradually began packing, to return home, before total darkness. Just then, police cars, with sirens blaring and lights flashing, raced along the highway, past the fading festivities.

They were heading for the mountains. Sami nervously helped speed up the process. He started to briskly load up Farhad's vehicle, so he could abandon the site quickly, tagging along with everyone else. Soon Farhad intervened, to emphasize that Sami was their guest of honor; to leave the work for Fatima, the family servant, cook and former nanny to Shevan--when he was an infant. In fact, she was like a second mother in the house. The rugs were rolled up and shoved into the station wagon. Utensils and leftovers were tucked in, by Farhad's driver, Hassan.

"Agha, we are ready to leave," said Hassan, addressing Farhad by his inherited honorary tribal title. Sami sidled up to Farhad.

"I must remember to address you properly, in Zakho," Sami whispered. Farhad laughed and told Sami to be himself, just like in the old days, at the Baghdad Jesuit high school.

As Hassan pulled away onto the highway, towards Zakho, Sami kept staring in the wagon's side-mirror. Then he fidgeted in his seat. US Air Force Colonel Sami noticed a patrol car behind, speeding towards them, from the mountain's direction. The police vehicle was approaching Farhad's station wagon, from the rear, at an uncomfortable clip, for Sami. Staring into the mirror, Sami saw Kurdish cops turn their auto off the road, into the remnants of wedding guests. They were still busy packing to get home. A sigh of relief lit up Sami's face. Farhad asked if he was sleepy. Tired but not sleepy, was Sami's ready reply, as he gazed at the fading sight, in the rear-view mirror.

Soon, the old windmill was in sight. Sami knew that they had arrived at Farhad's house. Even more amazed he was that same windmill still produced electricity and helped pump all the water they needed, from the Khaboor river. There was municipal water and electricity in Zakho but Farhad's household did not need it. Last time he was here, eons ago it seemed, Sami remembered the unreliable power from the one small source, which served the few hookups in the fifteen-thousand population of the day

"I know what you're thinking, Sami. I kept the windmill in memory of my dad. He was so creative, despite his lack of a science background," said Farhad wistfully.

"Haji Agha, may God bless his soul, was very smart and kind," chimed in Fatima, who had been hired by Farhad's dad, as an orphaned maid, ages ago. Farhad turned on the TV, maintaining conversation with Fatima.

"Didn't Bahri bring you to my Father's attention?" Farhad flipped through channels.

"My parents were taken away by government soldiers, and I was left alone to roam the streets," Fatima wiped a tear.

"Everyone was scared to help, except Bahri, the only black man in Zakho, a devout man and true Muslim," she continued. "He brought me to your kind father, and I've been part of this blessed household ever since," said Fatima.

The CNN channel showed a lot of serious faces in clergy garb. A Vatican official seemed to be eulogizing a great loss to the Catholic church. Trying to suppress his agitation, Sami suggested watching local programs, having missed Kurdish music and songs, all these years in America. Just before changing the channel, the TV anchorman barged in. He told the viewers he would be back after the break, for more interviews with Vatican personnel about the death of Urban IX.

"My God, the Pope is dead! That was Father Rogan; he taught me English at Baghdad Jesuit high," said Farhad as he sat in the lotus position, close to the TV set. Sami shifted uncomfortably in his seat, gazing at the screen absent-mindedly. A dropped pot in the kitchen woke colonel Sami Yusuf from his reverie. He crawled over to Farhad.

"Before news anchorman comes back, I would like to talk to you in private." Sami had a grim face on, which surprised Farhad. Switching off the TV set, Farhad lead him to his study.

Chapter 23--The Confession

FARHAD SEATED SAMI IN his chair, behind the desk, then pulled up another chair. He sat across, then looked sympathetically into Sami's troubled eyes.

"Just like old times at the Jesuit school. What is it, Sami?" said Farhad, renewing his role of friend and confidant.

"I don't know if you can handle this one. It is much more serious than Father Mahan's "no ticky, no cinny" rule. When I lost my cinema ticket, or cinny's ticky, he merely banned me from the next weekend movie, in downtown Baghdad." Sami dovetailed his fingers to stop them from visibly shaking. Sliding the chair closer, Farhad placed his hand on Sami's shoulder.

"Remember when Leon, the Christian bully, gave me alcohol at the Soiree, and tried to molest me in the rear?" said Farhad. Sami nodded. "When the potential scandal caught your eye, Sami, you lead Leon outside the building, then beat the hell out of the bastard." Farhad was getting emotional; "if the son-of-a-bitch had succeeded, I could not have lived here, facing my family every day, with that shame on my conscience." Farhad paused. "You saved me from killing Leon, to cleanse my honor, as well as our family name; you kept me out of jail. I owe you a big one, Sami." Farhad stopped and called Fatima to bring two istikan cups of tea, and some baqlava. Fidgeting in his seat, Sami just mumbled. A tear rolled down his cheek. Farhad urged him to speak freely, and get it off his chest.

"You said you owe me a big one. Right now I need a huge one," Sami looked down on the floor, evading Farhad's probing eyes. If Sami still considered him a friend, Farhad insisted that he spill it all out. Reaching for his istikan, Sami sipped some tea, then picked some lint off his clothing. That's where he ran out of delay tactics. Farhad was following every move Sami made, anxiously awaiting the story. Nervously rotating a pen, Sami stared at his shoes, which were degradation symbols, in Iraqi culture. He began moving his lips. In a society where honor and shame were the two sides of the coin of life-and-death, it was not easy to talk to a friend, at eye level.

"Do you remember that dusty overcast day in Baghdad, at the Jesuit boarding house?" began Sami. There were several such days; Farhad wished to know which one. "The day the president hanged all those people, including several Jews." Sami glanced at Farhad, who nodded. "Well Father Rogan was upset about all this, and invited me to his room, to ostensibly learn the Iraqi view. He was agonizing on how it would affect the Jesuits' future in the country." After a deep breath, Sami took a bite of baqlava. Seeing Farhad dying to hear more, he resumed. "There was a Johnny Walker whiskey bottle on his desk. He filled a glass and drank it, then refilled it and downed it again. He seemed troubled and upset," said Sami to the astonished Farhad. He had never seen a Jesuit drink in his presence. "Rogan then poured me a glass of the whiskey, added a little water, acting like it was a lot of water, and handed it to me: 'go on, I authorize you to take it!' So I see this Reverend Rogan smile, and promise me a good grade, if I gulped it down like a man," continued Sami.

"So what did you do?" gasped Farhad.

"I really needed a good grade in Rogan's class, so I drank the whole glass. He gave me another one, slurring his words. Shortly after, he took off his garb and threw it on the chair. He then lay on the bed and asked me to sit on the bedside and talk to him; that he was terribly homesick. So I did, being tipsy, I wasn't sure what I was doing. Do you really want to hear more?" Sami was not sure whether he should go on. Farhad was emphatic. There was no way he would let Sami leave him dangling like that. "Rogan then pulled me into his bed, undressed me and himself naked. He proceeded to excite both of us, like an ordinary deprived and depraved man." Sami paused and begged Farhad to excuse him; he could not go on. Farhad insisted on the whole story.

"Didn't you tell me once, that a true friend was one, who knew all about you and was still a friend?" Farhad patted the shoulder of Sami, who nodded in assent. "You screwed the bastard, of course, right?" said Farhad.

"That's the whole point; he did me in the rear, I'm ashamed to say," getting up to go: "I don't deserve to be your friend," said Sami, as he faced a persistent. Farhad pressed him back onto his seat.

"Knowing you, Sami, I'm sure this is not the whole story. You might as well finish it, " said Farhad.

"When you go back to watch CNN, you will soon see my picture," Sami paused as Farhad's jaw dropped.

"What did you do, for fuck's sake, Sami?" Farhad rose, rubbed his eyes, walked around the room, then came back and sat, staring. Sami got up, ready to leave. Farhad absolutely refused to let him go, and practically ordered him to sit down. He had to hear the ending, for one; and secondly, he knew how important it was for Sami, to unburden his troubled mind.

"You asked for it, my good friend, Frarhad. I killed the Pope," Sami banged on the table and started to cry. Farhad hugged him, handing him a Kleenex.

"You had to do it, Sami. How else could you face your father, with this shame hanging around your neck." Farhad helped dry Sami's tears. "I may not have liked to see you, had you not redeemed your family's honor, my dear honorable Sami." Farhad got up and paced the floor, then asked Sami how he pulled it off; and how on Earth he got to Zakho, without the US and NATO Air Forces on his tail.

"It's all on CNN. You're now ready to go watch it," said Sami, as he rose to exit the room with Farhad.

Chapter 24--On TV

IN THE LIVING ROOM, Farhad immediately turned on the TV, keeping the volume low. Besides Sami, there was no one else in the room. Though his household help knew no English, Farhad still did not want the wrong people outside the room to overhear. Not until he figured out how to handle this explosive situation, unfolding in his own home. Both sat on the carpet, near the television set, for the continuous coverage. It had displaced all regular programming. On-screen, was a shaky movie taken by some amateur cameraman. He had caught an American Air Force plane launching two missiles into the papal balcony.

"You did that?" Farhad turned to Sami in disbelief. Deep in thought, Sami nodded. "There's your picture," Farhad jumped onto his feet, pointing at the TV screen. Sami just stared, absent-minded. There was an all-points bulletin for the arrest of Colonel Sami Yusuf, AWOL from the United States Air Force, wanted for multiple murders, in connection with the assassination of Pope Urban IX, as well as two cardinals of the Roman Catholic church. A five-million dollar reward was also announced. Some eyewitnesses saw the plane fly eastward, after attacking the Vatican. Satellite photos tracked the Air Force plane, heading towards Incerlik, in Turkey. It never landed at that American airbase, and the search was on to locate the jet fighter.

There was a theory, that it must have crashed somewhere in the mountains of Turkey, but no one had yet located any wreckage. The same TV talking-head speculated, that this could turn out to be another D. B. Cooper legend.

"Good! They don't know where you are," said Farhad. That gives us time. "What would you like to do, Sami," Farhad put his arm around Sami's shoulder.

"Just to see Baba, before they take me away," sniffed Sami.

"You'll see your father, God willing, inshallah." Farhad was determined, that his old school buddy would have his wish. "We must get you to Baghdad safely, and then to dad's Mansur district," said Farhad pensively. "Fortunately, Mansur is not as bad as other areas, like Sadr City or Adhamia," he added, waving a Baghdad daily, bought from a Zakho newsstand. Farhad paced the floor, rubbing his forehead. "No matter how I look at it, my people must take you all the way to your father," said Farhad, still walking back and forth in the room. "With anyone else, greed may drive them straight to the US embassy, to collect those millions on your head. We're talking dollars, not cheap Iraqi dinars. These days, men will kill for half that figure in dinars, let alone dollars." Farhad sat down and awaited an opinion. It came fast: Sami had absolutely no right to subject Farhad to this kind of predicament. Farhad would have none of that, especially when he had done it to protect the family name--honor and life was one and the same in Iraq. That even in America, killing was permitted in self defense. The onus was on the Pope. Rogan received his just reward, Farhad reasoned.

"Priests are ordained to save souls, not molest the youth in their care!" Farhad thought that he had just uttered something more profound than he intended to. "They're soul doctors. A doctor must heal you, not make you sick," he added.

"Imagine all the years of heartache and mental torture they inflict on their victims, until Judgement Day and their date in Hell," Sami pointed down.

Reviewing the options, Farhad convinced Sami he could not go to Baghdad on his own. These were different times from when he was here last. Then, it was the tyranny of one ruler; now it was the terror of the lawless many.

They listened to the latest news on television. The plane Sami used, to attack the Vatican, was still being sought. It was yet to be located. That gave Sami a window of opportunity. He could reach Baghdad, before the US had reason to scour Kurdistan. It had great influence with the pro-American Kurds. Even a tribal leader, like Farhad, could not go against the wishes of the regional Kurdish government.

Chapter 25--ID's For A Perilous Journey

THERE WASN'T A MOMENT to lose, for the start of Sami's journey to Baghdad. It was a matter of time, before his abandoned American fighter plane would be found, and the location passed on to America. The United States could pull strings everywhere, to catch the AWOL Colonel Sami Yusuf, and charge him with triple murder, of the Holy Father and the two princes of the Roman Catholic church. Put that way, Sami would have no chance to see the light of day again. Having achieved his ultimate vendetta, the only other goal for Sami was to see Baba, his dear infirm dad, while both of them were still alive. For Sami, any days lived after seeing Baba, would be 'naam Allah', or God's bounty, in Iraqi vernacular.

Looking at his watch, Farhad called in Hassan, his chauffeur, butler and handyman. First thing in the morning, Hassan was to go to Abu Kamal, and obtain two identity cards for Sami: one with a Sunni name, like Omar, the other with a Shiite name like Ali. Waving a finger, Farhad ordered Hassan to get one for himself too--with a Sunni name on a fake ID card. He reminded Hassan that Arab Sunnis would not believe that he could possibly be a Sunni, with a Shiite name like Hassan. His puzzled driver asked what all this was about.

"You are driving Sami to Baghdad, as soon as you come back with those real-looking false documents," ordered Farhad. "It's the same route you took, to bring Aunt Amina here, from Baghdad, two years ago," Farhad was confident Hassan could do it, despite increased violence between some Sunni and Shiite communities. "Pay Abu Kamal double his fees, so he gets everything ready by tomorrow. After tomorrow, everyone will be off for the feast of Eid," Farhad spoke with grim urgency.

Abu Kamal became an expert forger during Baghdad's terror years. He had saved many a life, by helping desperate Kurds flee the country, with false papers. Several officials, running Kurdistan now, were still alive, thanks to Abu Kamal. That's why his little clandestine operation was still in business. Kurdish bureaucrats, thinking they may need his services again, in such fickle times, looked the other way, every time Abu Kamal's illicit business came up. With Turkey as a potential invader, and the central Baghdad government weak, Kurds had learned to keep all their options accessible at short notice.

It was a night of tossing and turning for Farhad. What if Sami or Hassan were kidnapped, say at a sham checkpoint? Should ransom rise beyond his means, what then? Topping all that, the US could force the Kurdish government to arrest him, for harboring a wanted American killer. Which way would he turn? What if he ended up in Guantanamo Bay and not heard of again? At every question, Farhad moaned then spun on the mattress.

At dawn, the muezzin, through loudspeakers, called the faithful to prayer. Farhad did the ritual washing, spread his rug on the floor, faced south towards Mecca, then prayed with all the supplication he could muster. Today, he asked God for a special favor: to protect Sami and Hassan, while traveling to Baghdad. On his knees, he turned his head to the left and to the right, cursing away the Devil. That gesture concluded the prayer. Putting away the prayer rug, Farhad slipped into bed for some sleep, before the hectic day that was certain to unfold.

Fatima walked in with a pot of tea and an istikan cup, and placed them on Farhad's bedside table. The rattles knocked him off his light sleep. He told her to wake Sami up with tea, then fetch breakfast for both, at about nine o'clock that morning. Hassan had already eaten, and was gone to Abu Kamal, she informed him. After breakfast, she was to pack lunch and dinner for Sami and Hassan, for their long trip to Baghdad. Farhad ordered Sami's favorite dish: the one he remembered, when they were roommates at the Jesuit school. It was the yogurt kubba, and it was sure to ease Sami's travel, Farhad figured, as he gave Fatima his instructions.

Which car to send to Baghdad, was the next dilemma for Farhad. The new Mercedes would be certain to attract potential kidnappers. They would no doubt weigh the owner's affordability towards a hefty ransom—much like US county assessors, who were familiar to Sami. The old Ford, on the other hand, would definitely not be a ransom target. But it was less reliable than the Mercedes, on a lengthy journey. He opted for the Ford. It would be more manageable, if things went wrong, especially with Hassan's untested experience and skills, at repairing cars. Clothing for Sami's trip was not a problem. He still fitted into Farhad's shirts and suits, as in the old days. Three items of every set were to be packed by Fatima, and readied for the trek north, as clearly instructed by Farhad.

The two were having breakfast when a call came in from Hassan. It was urgent that Abu Kamal have two passport photos of Sami, immediately. They would go on the ID cards that must be ready that same day.   Otherwise, they would have to wait till after the three-day festival of Eid. Hassan already had an extra photo snapped for himself. His Sunni-name ID was done. Quickly, Frahad dialed the nearest photographer. Unfortunately, he was away, buying the traditional Jordan almonds and gifts for the Eid. A call to another photographer was productive, and both got ready. Farhad lead Sami to Rassam's photo shop, a few blocks away.

On the wall hung a degree in photography from a college in Rome. Sami's heart sank, on seeing that city on the degree. For sure he thought the man had learned of the papal news, and could hand over his photo, if the Americans forced him to. Pulling Farhad to one side, Sami whispered his concerns. Rassam had been another terrorized Iraqi refugee in Italy. He would not betray another Kurd, Farhad assured Sami, as he sat for the photo. Within twenty minutes the pictures were ready, and the two rushed back home, to await Hassan. The excellent photographs would definitely enhance the authenticity of Sami's identity cards, Farhad figured, as he mulled them intently. It was not long before Hassan arrived, picked up the photos and returned to Abu Kamal for the ID cards. As an afterthought, Farhad decided that both Hassan and Sami ought to have an additional third ID each for neutral areas, or at check points of dubious or unknown affiliation.

Chapter 26--Leaving Zakho's Sanctuary

THE OLD FORD TAURUS wagon was packed, and ready for the long arduous journey to Baghdad. There was one final review of the plans and maps, which Farhad spread out over the table. Hassan would drive to Mosul, and avoid the trouble spots. Farhad marked every one of them on the city's map. Mosul was currently enjoying a peaceful spell. He then redlined the cities of Tikrit, Samarra and Baqubah, north of Baghdad. "Don't stop here, here or here to eat, shit, piss, or breathe. You should have enough food not to eat there. Beyond that, you're on your own, with your wits to guide you," Farhad rolled his eyes heavenward. "Zoom past these hellholes, even if you are crapping in your pants. Relieve yourselves on the road, past these crazy towns," said Farhad. He then went over the map of Baghdad and pointed at the suburb of Mansur. A tear rolled out of Sami's eye, as he mumbled 'Baba, I'm on my way', then sat down. Hassan got him a coke, while they all paused for a while. Taking a deep breath, Farhad put his arm around Sami's shoulder and pointed to the map.

"Mansur is still here. But it's almost like God picked it up and dropped it into a different city," Farhad resumed. "There's this fortified Green Zone on its east side, bordering the Tigris river, and the secured Baghdad airport not far west," said Frahad. "Perhaps that's why Mansur is safer than other places. But to get there is another matter," he looked at Hassan. "You have to follow the directions I've written here, and marked on the map, to the letter," Farhad told Hassan, grimly. "If you lose your way, ask where you are before you show any ID stuff." Farhad was still addressing Hassan, the driver. "In Sadr City or Kadhimiya, you are yourself, 'Hassan'; they don't know you're a Sunni Kurd with a revered Shiite name; Sami will use the Shiite 'Ali' card. In Sunni neighborhoods, you are Muhammad, and Sami is Omar, an unmistakable Sunni name; got it?" Farhad eyed the map then looked at Hassan, who signaled his agreement. "If you're not sure of the area, pull your neutral card. You are then Muhammad," he told Hassan. "There, Sami stays 'Sami', as on the Iraqi ID card," Farhad emphasized. "Be sure to put each card in a separate pocket or spot in the car. That way, you don't shuffle a bunch of ID's, while someone is watching." Farhad then exchanged cell and home phone numbers with Sami, including his father's, in Baghdad. Sami was not sure it was still valid. In any case he intended to surprise his dad with a totally unexpected visit. After all, he had just cleansed the family honor, having been besmirched by Father Rogan. Now, as the dead pope, he paid for sodomizing Sami at Baghdad Jesuit high. Steeped in Iraqi customs and culture, to Sami this was a timeless sin and crime, which the passing years could not ameliorate. Like dirty clothes, they would not get clean by themselves. He he had to do the job himself.

The two school friends hugged and kissed on both cheeks, in the age-old Middle Eastern tradition.

"Please give my respects to your father; let him know that we pray for his good health everyday," Farhad waved goodbye, as Sami and Hassan entered the car, and banged the doors shut. Sami waved back, as Hassan pulled away in the old blue Taurus, sending a little dust in the direction of a pensive Farhad. He stood there in deep thought, even after the car turned out of sight. The car was now on its way, up the road through the old Kaista neighborhood of Zakho, towards the twisting gully road, through the towering Bekhair mountains, heading for Mosul. At left, Sami could see an ancient arched stone bridge, some distance away. It exuded Roman architecture.

"Oh, that's the Abbassid bridge," Hassan explained. Sami wondered if the Abbasid Caliphate had built it, before the Monguls destroyed Baghdad, in the thirteenth century. Recalling a visiting scholar, Hassan relayed that it was constructed by an Ottoman bridge builder, named Abbas.

The mountains were lush and green, this time of year, with a brook here and a stream there, occasionally running over a waterfall. Puzzled as to why they named it 'Bekhair', when these mountains looked so fertile.

"True, the word bekhair means barren in Kurdish, but who knows what condition these tall mountains were in, when named Bekhair, ages ago," said Hassan; "the butcher of Baghdad rendered these highlands true to their name, during his destruction of Kurdistan, and our people," Hassan slowed down for a man on a donkey, crossing the road.

Chapter 27--Mosul Stopover

THE CAR RADIO SPRAYED them with Baghdad news. It was not good, especially for travelers heading that way. Sectarian killings between Sunnis and Sadr City Shiites, were getting more brutal. It was too depressing and scary to hear. If Hassan turned around now, heading back to Zakho, before Sami could see his dad, Farhad would be very upset. So he switched the radio to a station with peppy Kurdish music. Sami snapped his fingers in tune, as Hassan stayed on course.

"Kurdish songs and dancing always cheered me up, going back to my first visit to Farhad, so long ago," mused Sami.

The trip was uneventful for a good while, with a rare routine checkpoint, manned by friendly Peshmerga Kurdish soldiers. Makeshift halting spots started to appear, and gradually got more frequent, as well as thorough. The old Ford was now in the Arab-ruled Nineveh province, though still in Kurdish territory.

"This means we're near Mosul," said Hassan. " A former Baghdad ruler had taken vast Kurdish lands, and annexed them to this Arab-dominated province, which was ruled by his henchmen from Mosul," Hassan stopped again for another check. Cards, with their real names on, worked fine. There were only a few Shiites in northern Iraq, for Sunni Arabs to bash. The threat here was sabotage and destructive terrorism, against oil pipelines and infrastructure. It was intended to disrupt the Shiite majority government in Baghdad. "They used to call Mosul, the City of Two Springs, because the Autumn was as beautiful as the Spring," said Hassan. "The city was a tenth of today's size. My father used to visit uncle Kassem in October or November. In less than twenty minutes, his antique English Standard car would leave the city behind, into lush green fields, for a great picnic." Hassan turned grim. "That was before the Mosul thugs of the dictator took him away, and killed him. If I know where uncle Kassem is buried, I would place his favorite roses on the grave." Hassan was now inside Mosul's borders.

"There's the leaning minaret. Now I know we're in Mosul," Sami pointed with excitement.

"That's why many Muslawis call Mosul the 'Leaning City'," joined in Hassan.

"Reminds me of the Leaning Tower of Pizza," said Sami. "The Italians are trying to prevent it from falling down. What are they doing to save this minaret?" Sami glanced at Hassan.

"The tyrant of Baghdad and his hit men were too busy destroying everything. It never occurred to them to save anything, except their rule and their skin." Hassan was now driving past the historic minaret. He then took a little detour past an old mansion, which now appeared to be a police station

"That was Dr. Stergian's house. He saved my life when I was a kid," said Hassan. Sami wanted to know what was an Armenian doctor doing in Mosul, and what about Zakho doctors? Hassan explained that during the forced Armenian migration by the Ottomans during World War I, many of them took refuge in

Mosul and Kurdistan. Among those Armenians were the parents of Dr. Stergian, who was one of the best doctors in Iraq, at the time. Zakho, then, had only one doctor, Wadi. Its population, then, was about fifteen thousand. He was not a specialist, Hassan explained. "So, Haji Agha, Farhad's father prevailed over my dad, to send me on a long trip past the mighty Bekhair mountains all the way to Mosul, just to see Dr. Stergian." Hassan had a nostalgic smile on his face. In fact his father had little choice, being his lifelong servant. "But he cured me of malaria, and I was back in Zakho in a short time," said Hassan. "After that, Haji Agha's words were as good as the Quran. May Allah bless his soul." Hassan wiped a tear.

A gas station loomed, and Hassan decided it was a good time and place to fill up. He then pulled out Farhad's instructions. They were to spend the night at Amina's, Farhad's favorite aunt. The directions were clear to the Dawasa district, where she had lived all her life. Amina greeted them with her usual hospitality, despite her frailty. She had a black headband, and wore a black dress, as was the lifetime custom for widows. They would never remarry, once the husband had been recalled by God, in Hassan's words. Social custom required that the widow stay single, and in mourning till death, explained Hassan later, to Sami. She sent her servant to shop for the best cuts of meat and vegetables he could find. Her visiting daughter soon cooked a sumptuous meal. Amina had a lot of questions about Farhad. He had not been able to visit her in years. She understood that it had been tough for Kurdish men to travel and visit relatives, with the type of rulers Iraq had, until the regime was toppled, by the grace of Allah, as Amina put it. She recalled the old days when Haji Agha would come to Mosul and bring her a bagful of grouse, which he had hunted, around Zakho's villages. This was before Baghdad's tyrant destroyed those towns, in the anti-Kurdish campaign.

"We would eat cooked grouse for a week, then give the rest to our neighbors," Amina recalled the days of a bygone era, like it was a dream. She was making plans for lunch and dinner for the following day, but was disappointed to learn that Sami and Hassan were to leave early next morning. She called Farhad in Zakho. She demanded to know why he was imposing this hardship on these two good people, as she audibly complained to Farhad. He told Aunt Amina, that Sami needed to see his sick father. No one knew how long he would live.

"Let Sami see his father before he dies. It would burden your conscience, if he missed this opportunity," Fahrhad's pleading voice crackled on the phone.

"Alright, but they will have the same breakfast, lunch and dinner on the way, as they would have here at my home, " said Amina as she hung up.

Chapter 28--Where Tyrant's Sons Died

DAWN OF THE NEXT day was announced through the muezzin's loudspeakers, calling the faithful to prayer. Amina turned on the radio. It always started with passages from the Quran. This morning the selected verses were about all Muslims being brothers.

"So who gave the Baghdadi Muslims a permit to kill other brother Muslims? Did you kill your brother?" Sami looked at Hassan. He was spreading his prayer rug. Hassan shot back that those creatures were not Muslims, but criminals hiding behind a faith of goodness, mercy and peace. After his ritualistic obligation, Hassan offered Sami his personal rug, to pray on. Secular, and privately agnostic, Sami politely declined. He explained that he was not clean enough, inside, to face God in prayer. Perhaps he would start after pilgrimage to Mecca. He earnestly hoped that it would close the subject.

The radio's Quran reading was followed by broadcast news. Everyone expected to hear about another round of sectarian revenge killings in Baghdad, inflicted by Muslims on fellow Muslims, in total violation of the holy scriptures. Instead, the top headline was the killing of a Christian leader in the West. Amina walked into the living room with a hurried shuffle.

"What is the world coming to! It says the Pope has been assassinated." Amina was agitated. "Did you hear that? They still don't know who did it," she looked at Sami. "Wasn't he the one who taught Farhad at that Baghdad Christian school? I begged his father to put him in a good Islamic madrasa." Amina's headgear flaps swung from side to side. "He refused, insisting on sending Farhad to the best school he could find, even if it was run by Satan!" Amina straightened her head scarf. "So how good is a madrasa run by infidels, I ask you?" She sat down, as Sami feigned agreement. His mind was elsewhere. He sighed in relief, when the Vatican attacker was not shown here. He would have an awful time escaping Amina's interrogation. She kept waving a finger at her dead brother, for sending Farhad to a heathen place, to learn from the devil, as she put it. She had very much wanted Farhad to memorize the Quran in a fine Muslim school.

"The Pope was my teacher too at the Baghdad school. I shared a room with Farhad, over there; didn't he tell you, Aunt Amina?" Sami's mind was elsewhere, with a look of shock at the papal news. So many things were told to Amina over the years, that she wished it would all come back. Now it would be pure luck, if she could remember which pill to take next. Sami walked over and hugged Amina tenderly, thanking profusely for her hospitality, and all that food in the car, to tide them over the long journey. Eyeing Hassan, he was now ready to resume the trip to Baghdad.

"I don't know your father, but tell him this little woman in Mosul is praying to Allah for his safety and wellbeing," Amina wiped a tear, sentimental as always. She still had not recovered from losing her husband and brother, Farhad's father, even though it has been years since they passed away.

The old Ford Taurus rounded the corner and out of sight. Amina waved, then slowly closed her front door, mumbling prayers to Allah. She then rolled her eyes up, pleading with the heavenly Listener to protect them, so Sami could see his sick father "before You, the Supreme Creator, recall him to your side," Amina supplicated, pulling her holy beads vigorously, one by one around a circular nylon string. While looking up in prayer, Amina's eyes caught the wall clock. It was ten after eight that crisp sunny morning. From her long experience of seeing off relatives, she figured that Sami and Hassan should make it to Baghdad before dark. That was her best estimate. She was not much good at calculating time and distance to the n-th degree, as the Jesuits had taught her nephew, Farhad, in their Baghdad school.

Before they were out of Mosul, Sami wanted very much to drive past the house where the dictator's two sons and a grandson met their fate. They faced a superior American force. Thus ended a reign that terrorized Sami's dad, along with other Baghdadis. Hassan did not know how to find the structure. Nor did he think it safe to ask around for directions, in Sunni Mosul. Many activists had come here to hide. In fact it was not necessary to ask. Sami had saved up magazine clippings of the military operation, which included the neighborhood map, and even the address. Being familiar with Mosul, Hassan just needed the name of the district and of the street. He could then drive him to the dreadful-duo's final refuge. Sami shuffled some newspaper clippings, pulling out a Los Angeles Times report. He told Hassan to drive to Shalalat Street, in the well-to-do al-Fatah neighborhood. Knowing that area, Hassan headed straight for the street. Looking at published photos of the house, Sami shouted: "there's the villa". He asked Hassan to park a while across the street from the infamous house of the so-called friend of the sons of the deposed tyrant. He had sold them out to the Americans, for fifty million dollars--twenty five apiece. "A highly profitable trade indeed, for a dual scum," Sami thought. He sat silently in the car, mulling over the significance of it all. Sami then juxtaposed dead killer sons in that house, in his mind, to all the havoc they had wreaked on his dear old Baba and other Baghdadis, for seemmingly endless years. Hassan saw it differently, reminding Sami that the tyrant's sons fought bravely to death,. In contrast, their father, cowered in a spider hole, till uncovered by Americans.

Sami took a deep breath, then told Hassan to head for Baghdad and the Mansur district. As the car pulled away, Sami's eyes were transfixed on that house, until it was out of sight. He couldn't wait to tell Baba that he saw the spot, where famous duo's terror finally came to an end. But, being Iraq, a new kind of terror had reared its head. It was called sectarian revenge. Sami was not anxious to hear any of that from his dad, in his sick bed at home. The house was smack-dab inside the mixed Sunni-Shiite neighborhood of Mansur. It was also close to the fortified, often-targeted Green Zone, in the heart of Baghdad. It also meant that the area was a little safer than the rest of the city. Even then, it was nothing to write Luke about--way over in San Francisco, where he truly felt at home.

Chapter 29--Risky Stretch to Tikrit

BARRING BREAKDOWN OF THE car or the law, Hassan estimated a Mansur arrival time of no later than 6 p.m., allowing for gas, bathroom and refreshment breaks, along the way. Thanks to Amina's bountiful packed cuisine, there was no need to stop over at slow-service restaurants on the way. That saved them much travel time. In any case, they were not to stop anywhere near Balad, Bayji, Tikrit, Samarra or Baquba. Otherwise, Hassan would have a lot of explaining to do for Farhad, if and when he was back in Zakho. These towns were strongholds of militant Sunnis. Here, lawless elements were trying to stir a sectarian grudge match with the Shiites. Outside of Mosul, Hassan pulled over, opened a secret floor compartment in the Ford wagon. There, he had hidden all but Sunni-friendly identifying documents. Items locked away included Hassan's true ID card. He was a Kurdish Sunni with the Shiite name of Hassan, which he could not easily explain away. The fanatics of the Sunni Triangle would never understand that the Kurds revered all Muslim holy men of the past, whether presently revered or reviled by Shiites or Sunnis.

Getting back in the driver's seat, Hassan waited for a sheep herd to cross the road. Ahead was a shepherd in Kurdish garb, with a hood over his head. Moving past the flock, Hassan voiced a greeting in Kurdish. The shepherd responded in kind, straightening his turban, under the hood. His shoe soles were cut from used tires. Their threads revealed a lot of walking mileage, behind his grazing sheep. Sami wondered out loud, whether shepherds engaged in feuds, or ran away from anything.

"These people have no luxury of time that city folks indulge in," smiled Hassan. "They just run away from dry grass to green grass. Nothing else matters to them." Hassan pressed a little more on the accelerator. Soon the sheep were dots in the rearview mirror, as the old Taurus sped southward.

Passing the Balad sign, they had to halt at what appeared to be a police checkpoint, next to a demolished military vehicle-- still smoldering. Upon showing the Sunni ID cards, Hassan was waved on. Sami kept listening to the news. He was anxious to learn if he was yet identified, by name, as the Pope's assassin. No such information crackled on the airwaves yet.

It has been now about two hours since Amina's emotional goodbye in Mosul. The road sign confirmed that they were in the vicinity of Bayji. Here, an oil pipeline to Turkey had been a repeated target by anti-government saboteurs. The sound of gunfire, ahead of them, caught Hassan and Sami by surprise. At a distance, along the road, south of them, they could make out a north-bound pickup truck. It was being chased by a military SUV, with guns blazing from both vehicles. Sami looked at Hassan, as to what to do about this mayhem, heading in their direction. Always quick-witted, Hassan stopped dead on the road's shoulder, and immediately leaped out of the car. He signaled at Sami to follow him. Both jumped into a roadside ditch, and laid low. They soon heard the sound of zooming bullets grow louder and louder, maxing out at their hideout, before passing and fading away.

Rising slowly from the ditch, Hassan and Sami looked north. By now, the racing vehicles looked like mere specks. They rushed to the aging Ford wagon, and walked around it. There were no flat tires, to their great relief. Then they anxiously checked the car for any damage. There was a hole in the windshield. A bullet had pierced the hood. Lifting it, they saw a dangling fan belt, sliced by the projectile. Hassan went to the box of spare parts, grabbed a belt and quickly replaced the damaged one. As they got ready to enter the car, the battling SUV reappeared coming back their way. It stopped behind the Taurus. Two handcuffed men, with Arab kaffiyeh headdress, sat dejectedly in the rear of the military vehicle. An Iraqi soldier jumped out and offered help. He apologized for the holes from bullets that had strayed into the Ford. Showing the soldier the damaged fan belt, Hassan told him he had just put a new one in, and the old wagon should deliver them to their destination. He thanked the uniformed man for his concern. He also expressed how refreshing a change Hassan noticed from the old attitude of the military, who never used to care if they hurt or killed innocent citizens.

The SUV screeched off, continuing in its southerly direction. After it disappeared, Hassan resumed the journey to Baghdad. Sami recalled reading, in US publications, about how Americans had trained Iraqis in law enforcement. It included treating the public with respect, so they would cooperate with lawmen.

"This nice soldier must've done his homework, and passed his exam," Sami smiled.

Open flat fields spread out to great distances, on both sides
of the road. The asphalt highway, stretching ahead of them,
could be seen for miles, ending in a mirage, in the afternoon
heat. This hazy image seemed to move ahead of them, as they
kept driving southward. Several miles later, they saw figures
moving in the mirage, way out in the distance, as their Taurus
wagon passed Tikrit's road sign. Not sure what to do, Hassan
slowed down. He needed to assess the situation, before passing
the area of apparent activity. Gradually a parked ambulance
materialized, with medics carrying injured people on stretchers,
to the Red-Crescent van. A badly-damaged army truck lay
next to the hospital vehicle. An official was waving traffic on,
hurrying up rubber-neckers.

Sami asked what had happened. The official had only time
to mention RPG. It was clear enough to Sami, being a military
man himself. He did translate it to the puzzled Hassan, as
Rocket Propelled Grenade. Baathist insurgents were active here
in Tikrit. It was the birthplace of their hero, the deposed ruler.
Both of them were relieved that this violent event concluded
before their arrival. Also, the map told them they had passed
the halfway mark from Mosul to Baghdad. It reminded Sami of
a Roman general, crossing the Rubicon river. It was the point
of no-return, on their way to a military campaign. History
fascinated Sami, ever since learning that Hammurabi had
created the world's first body of laws for the Babylonians. Their
empire was centered in ancient Iraq.

"How ironic," Sami glanced at Hassan. "Iraq invented the
law, thousands of years ago, and there is no law, today, in Iraq,
where it was first posted, right here in ancient Mesopotamia!"
declared Sami. He had fallen back again into lecture mode, as
when he trained pilots in the US Air Force, in California and

Aviano, Italy. Though a recent instructor, to Sami it was like it happened eons ago. That before his plane had crossed vast expanses of water, on the way to Iraq.

Chapter 30--Close Call in Samarra

AFTER TIKRIT, THE TRIP was uneventful for a good stretch of road. The fuel gauge was edging close to E, on the front panel. It displayed the sketch of a gas pump, to warn of a near-empty tank. Hassan was ready for the next exit, to restock on 'panzene', the local name for gasoline. It was another opportunity for Sami to talk history. When the first cars arrived in Iraq, early in the twentieth century, they ran on benzene, a petroleum derivative, before the refiners settled on gasoline. An exit loomed some distance ahead. When they got closer, to their dismay, the highway exit sign read 'Samarra'. The city had been specifically ruled out by Farhad. He had warned Hassan and Sami, that the Shiite minority, here, were still mad at the Sunnis for blowing up their centuries-old golden-domed mosque and shrine. It was a deliberate act of sacrilege, to provoke Iraq's ruling majority Shiites into a civil war. In the ensuing chaos, the culprit, a minority of religious fanatics, would then grab power, reasoned Farhad.

The Ford wagon paused by the roadside for a spell, so Hassan and Sami could discuss what to do. There were two impossible options. Sami compared it to an unstoppable force approaching an immovable object. They had to choose between entering a dangerous city, with possible fatal consequences. Or they would continue driving until they ran out of gas. It could be in no-man's-land, at the mercy of kidnappers or insurgents. Hassan called Farhad on the cellphones, for approval to enter Samarra. The crackling voice from Zakho asked if he had already used the two gallons in the spare emergency can.

"Not yet," said Hassan. "I want to save it for a dire emergency, like escaping from an erupting battle zone, or take a long route around a car-bombed area." Hassan looked at Sami. He nodded approval. Farhad recalled that Hassan's past judgments and decisions had been good, except for a couple of near-fatal ones.

"There are two lives in your hands, Hassan. Use your common sense, and you should all come of it safe and sound, inshalla, God willing." Farhad hung up just as his dog barked, heralding the arrival of a guest at his Zakho mansion. Putting the cellphones in the Ford's glove compartment, he sat silently for a few moments, eyeing Sami occasionally. Then he asked Sami what he thought they should do. As a US Air Force pilot, Colonel Sami Yusuf had made some tough decisions, but none this dicey, he told Hassan. When the chips were down, Sami never ran away from a trouble spot. Here and now, of course, it was Samarra. Ironically, to sami, this red-flag name was an abbreviation of the city's original name: Surra-mun-ra'a, meaning, in classical Arabic, 'Joy-to-behold'. That was when the Abbasid caliph moved the capital to Samarra, in 836 AD, to supplant Baghdad for fifty six years.

"If I had to decide, I would go into Samarra and get my gas," said Sami, with a wistful historical recollection; "but it's all up to you, Hassan."

Shifting the old wagon's lever, Hassan put it in gear as the spinning tires kicked dust off the road's shoulder. At the exit, he turned and headed for downtown Samarra. Missing, was the gleaming golden dome of the Shiite mosque. Sami thought that dome-less Samarra was like New York City with no twin towers. It was a little disorienting for Sami. He missed the landmark that guided him, the last time he had visited Samarra, several years before. Then he spotted the lofty spiral minaret of al-Malwiya, which instantly re-oriented him. Much as he wanted, he could not visit this historic structure that overlooked the ruins of the Great Mosque. The Caliph al-Mutawakkil had built it in 850 AD, when Samarra was the capital of the Abbasid Caliphate.

The Ford Taurus turned into the first gas station Hassan saw. Driving past the window, they noticed the manager reading a publication, which looked like the holy book of Quran. A sign at the door announced the visit of Ayatollah Ali Alhussaini, a well-known fiery Shiite cleric. Without braking, Hassan continued to drive straight out of that gas station, to look for a safer refueling stop. The next one was a smaller one, with two rows of double pumps. A young smiling guy manned the station. He was in blue jeans and wore a baseball cap, with the San-Francisco-Giants logo on it. For a second, Sami felt at home, recalling his favorite team. When asked about it, the attendant whispered, that the cap was sent to him by his uncle from America. Sami decided they were in a friendly oasis.

Halfway through filling the tank, a military truck stopped at the second row of pumps, to stock up. The soldier stuck the nozzle in, and pumped. A few minutes later, Hassan was ready to leave. The Ford wagon entered the street, when a VW van screeched to a halt, beside the army vehicle. Two men, in Arab headgear and dishdashas, Iraqi men's dresses, rushed to the army truck. One man pulled the gas nozzle off the soldier's hand, sprayed gasoline all over the soldier and the government vehicle. The second man threw a lighted match at the gas-soaked soldier. The two men instantly jumped into the van, and zoomed past Farhad's Ford, leaving behind a huge blaze. Hassan and Sami barely escaped with their lives, as they witnessed huge explosions, while racing for the highway, towards Baghdad.

Chapter 31--Baghdad in Sight

PULLING OUT THE CELLPHONES from the car's glove compartment, Hassan decided to call Farhad about their safe exit from Samarra. He saved the harrowing details of the escape for when, or if, he ever got back to Zakho. There was no need to worry Farhad right now. Sami made no phone calls of his own. He wanted to surprise his father, for one. More importantly, Sami did not want to be traced through cellphones calls. He expected a massive manhunt, as soon as the world had learned that American pilot, Colonel Sami Yusuf, had murdered the Pope. Photos would, no doubt, pop up everywhere, with a lucrative bounty on his head. He knew, full well, that the US, Italy and high-tech countries would cooperate to locate him, through global positioning and other technology. Because Osama Bin Laden dumped his cellphoness, no one found him for years, figured Sami; even though he was no emulator of this Islamic fanatic--being secular himself. His vendetta against the Pope was not religious, but a cleansing, as he put it, of family honor. Being penetrated in the anus, was an unforgivable violation of himself and his family's name. This was doubly aggravated in

Iraqi culture, because the violator was also a Christian infidel, as viewed in Muslim society.

Seeing the sign to Taji, Sami knew he was not far from Baghdad and dear old Baba, after so many years. His Adam's apple bobbed up and down, as Sami went into a nostalgic reverie. It did not last long. He was jolted into reality, by the sound of an explosion. Traffic suddenly slowed down. They waited to pass by a badly damaged five-ton truck, that had run over a roadside bomb. Half a dozen wounded soldiers were waiting for ambulances. Other officers speeded up traffic. A Medi-Vac helicopter hovered above, to transfer two badly injured uniformed men to intensive care facilities.

It occurred to Sami that his trip to Baghdad was so much like playing Russian roulette. In fact, Luke had told him in San Francisco, that his dad played it when he was a soldier in Asia. He was desperate for money, to help his mom forestall foreclosure on their Palo Alto home. In a fit of depression, he took bets in a sleazy, secret city dive. Money was collected and the winnings were dished out in cash, by a greedy local entrepreneur. Fortunately, Luke's father got the empty bullet chamber three times. He then quit, and walked off with just enough cash to save their Bay Area house. Luke barely missed being fatherless and homeless, along with his mom. The Ford wagon passed the wounded soldiers. Sami and Hassan had just dodged the bullet from the Taji chamber, in this riskier Iraqi roulette. The struck-soldiers' luck had just run out, near Taji. It resulted in a strange reprieve, enabling Sami to see his dad, before his luck ran out too.

As they traveled further south, traffic got denser, and directional signs more frequent. Many were bigger, and pointed to Baghdad and its sprawling suburbs. But none of them advised, as to which road was safe for Sunnis to take, nor any paths recommended for Shiite drivers. Sami and Hassan were now on their own, to go by their wits, their ethnic map, and Farhad's notes about Baghdad's neighborhoods. Some of their information was already out of date, due to the ongoing religious cleansing by the two main sects of the Islamic religion. Mansur was safer and more stable than other districts of the capital. Fewer violent incidents had been reported in the news. How to get there, was the billion-dinar question, which Sami and Hassan were desperate to know the answer for.

To Sami, the old Ford became a little think tank. It resembled a mini-Hoover institution of Palo Alto, near the home of Luke. He always had handy solutions, for Sami's intricate problems. Right now, even Luke's brain was not available, for Sami to pick on, as in the old intimate, peaceful days of San Francisco. He quit calling it Baghdad-by-the-Bay. Instead, he dreamed of the day, when he could refer to his Baghdad as 'San Francisco by the Desert'. But here and now, he had to figure out a way to dodge bullets, before he could get to his dear old Baba, in Mansur. Sami pushed out all those irrelevant thoughts that always found their way into his mind, at the wrong moments. Perhaps it was a mental safety valve. Such thoughts, like why a Baghdadi called his dad 'Baba', while westerners used papa. Was it because the Arabic language lacked the letter 'p'? He skipped that question for now, to answer a life-or-death question: how to get to Mansur; and in one piece?

What if they followed a military truck going in their direction? Sami wondered out loud to Hassan. But, he had a question of his own: what if the soldiers mistook them for suicide bombers?

"Do you think those jittery soldiers would let us come close, so they get blown up to smithereens?" Hassan shook his head in an emphatic negative gesture.

Chapter 32--Perilous Plans to Mansur

THE BLUE TAURUS WAGON got off the busy thoroughfare. It found its way to a small, unobtrusive chai khana, an Iraqi teahouse-- equivalent to an American cafe. One difference: it was socially acceptable to lob seeds of sunflower, watermelon, or whatever, into one's mouth, crack them open, eat the kernels, then spit out the shells onto the dirt ground. Sami and Hassan picked a table as far away from falling shells as possible. The waiter escorted them to a corner rickety table, with chairs that wobbled over the uneven floor. Being typical furniture, they did not complain or seek another table. Also, from that vantage point, Hassan could keep an eye on Farhad's automobile. The layout of the chai khana was unusual, even for an Iraqi teahouse. Although the customer area was spacious, there were only about five tables. Most of them stood vacant.

The place resembled an outdoor extension of a small corner-building, where the food plates were coming from. Above was a roof that looked like a flat, solid tent cover, with sides descending to the ground, like windowless walls. At the entrance side, there was no gate. A big gap in the wall acted as the main entrance. A brook ran through the middle of the teahouse. Inside, water flowed in a concrete ditch. A small upstream overpass was reminiscent of a mini-bridge, in a Japanese garden. There was no crossover at the downstream end of the café. This was where food and drinks were prepared, across the cement rivulet, opposite the waiting customers. Whenever a client visibly waved his hand for service, the waiter would pace all the way to the overpass. He would then walk back downstream, on the client side of the brook, all the way to the customer. It reminded Sami of the Hyatt Regency in San Francisco, with its make-believe outdoor scene, indoors. He remembered a baseball sportscaster describing a new covered sports stadium, as the great indoors.

Only one man wore the local dishdasha male dress with a kaffiyeh covering his head. Everyone else in the teahouse was in regular pants and shirts. There were no religious posters, or rousing political speeches on the radio. Absent too, was the news about the Pope's death or any suspects. Sami was greatly relieved. The atmosphere here appeared less menacing. They did notice the manager talking to his son, who promptly sneaked around the Taurus wagon with a dog. From his military experience, Sami knew the canine had been trained to sniff out gunpowder and the like. Completing the circle around Farhad's car, the teenager shook his head sideways, at his father. It signified that his cafe was likely to survive for another day. Assured that the old Ford was not hiding deadly material, the manager ordered a waiter to serve Sami and Hassan. Their menu featured Iraqi kebab, which Sami had not eaten in over ten years. He was dying to taste it again. This was no San Francisco shish kebab. Spicy meat-dough was pressed around a thin metal spit, called shish, and placed over a bed of hot coals in a manqal. This was a rectangular iron container, full of flaming cinders. The spits rested on the end walls of the manqal. The kebab came with a side dish of tomatoes, green and white onions, along with distinctive Baghdad white bread rolls, known as samon, and pronounced 'summoon'. Each roll was oval shaped with two pointed ends, and preferred hot, fresh out of the bakery.

Hassan and Sami were now ready to go over the options, for the last leg of this long harrowing trip. Being on the outskirts of Baghdad, it was a matter of deciding which route was the safest, for travel to Mansur; and then onto Sami's boyhood home. His pilgrimage would end, when Sami had finally had seen his father. He did not care what happened to him after that. He was, however, concerned about Hassan getting back to Zakho safely; especially, after risking his life to do this favor for Sami. They examined the map and notes, as though innocent travelers. They were careful not to appear as conspirators. To the owner, these were unpredictable strangers. So Hassan and Sami pretended to be enjoying the drab scenery, whenever the proprietor looked in their direction. Both wearing non-descript pants and shirts, they did not arouse unusual suspicion.

The two tired riders agreed to stick to busy roads, as much as they could. This would make it difficult for anyone to take aim at them, in such a crowded area. If, by chance, they were near a target, then whatever happened would be the wish of Allah, as Hassan put it. Sami hoped, that they would not face the loaded-bullet chamber, in their deadly game of Iraqi roulette. In any case, they planned to drive to Al-Rashid street, going through mixed neighborhoods, in a southerly direction. At Haidar Khana mosque, they would turn right, go over the Tigris river, cross Haifa street, onto Cairo street. It all came back into Sami's memory. Just past Zawra and Park Zoo, that old right turn, always put him onto Mansur street. Then the left turn, shortly after Khair road, should take Sami to Baba and his boyhood home. A tear welled in Sami's eye, like it was all a dream. His mother was the big bonus; he did not have to prove anything to her. She was always in his corner, despite all family-honor taboos.

Chapter 33--Ominous Interruption

"WHAT COULD GO WRONG in the one percent of the trip, that's left?" said Sami, anxiously looking at Hassan, as they got into their auto, for the last leg of Sami's odyssey. Soon they were on Al-Rashid street, Baghdad's main thoroughfare. It was jammed to a crawl, just like Sami had always remembered it. Still, they were only a few blocks from the Haidar Khana mosque, where they would get off this street. Two men on a motorcycle passed their car. The rear passenger had a full satchel on his back. Hassan thought that the cyclists had the best idea, in this turtle-slow traffic. But, ten cars or so, ahead of them, they saw a blinding flash, accompanied by a loud bang. Then a wounded soldier hurried past the Taurus wagon. He paused by an acquaintance, on the sidewalk. He told them that their recruits' bus was destroyed by an explosive device. Two men placed the bomb under the vehicle, and quickly escaped on a motorcycle. Half his colleagues were dead, he said, as he left to get help. To Sami, it signified another empty bullet chamber in this Iraqi roulette, which they were unwittingly playing. He looked up to whoever was running the universe, begging Him to keep his good luck going for just a few more miles. "He's over there--my father; let me see him. Is that too much to ask?" Sami pleaded with the Almighty, just in case He existed.

With intimate knowledge of this area, from his early years, Sami knew how to bypass Al-Rashid street. He directed Hassan through a complicated array of side streets and alleyways. Some were barely wide enough for this Ford. A dozen left-right-left directions were animated to Hassan. It lead them to a bridge over the Tigris river. Crossing Haifa onto Cairo street, Sami took a deep breath. He felt he was almost there. His anxiety rose a few more notches at the junction of Zaitun, Damascus and Mansur streets. Hassan turned right into Mansur street, when Sami told him to stop on the road shoulder for a few minutes. He wanted to catch his breath, and collect his thoughts. The meeting was imminent, and Sami wasn't sure what he was going to say to his father after all these years. Not His mother. With Mama no such preparations were needed. Sami wanted to show off his rank as a colonel in the Air Force of the United States of America, which Baba had always admired. Hassan put away all the fake IDs in the Taurus' secret compartment, located in the wagon's rear floor. Putting his true identification in his pocket, Hassan handed Sami his real American ID card, which he tucked into his trousers pocket.

Hassan turned on the radio for some soft calming music. Instead, a bulletin was being broadcast for the arrest of Colonel Sami Yusuf, as the Pope's suspected murderer. Right then, a military convoy approached from the rear, then passed them by, to their great relief. The convoy turned left into his father's street, and his heart sank.

"They're looking for me. I don't know if my father can withstand the shock." Sami looked at Hassan, with desperate eyes. Immediately turning the car around, Hassan sought a temporary haven, if there was such a thing. These were violent times in Baghdad. Parking outside a house would arouse suspicion from armed owners. They stopped off the street, by Zawra park, to gather their wits and plan out the next move. Evening was approaching, and there was little time for decisions, being dangerous enough during daylight hours.

A VW wagon, with dark tinted windows, screeched to a halt in front of Farhad's Ford, at a blocking angle. Two armed men emerged, opened the front Taurus doors, and thrust AK-47 guns into their ribs. Sami and Hassan were ordered into the Volkswagen, then pushed onto the rear floor of the VW. Climbing, after Hassan and Sami, each gunman pinned down one of them, with their feet, and whacked their torsos with the gun butts. When either one tried to explain, they received a painful jab in the ribs. Their mouths were taped shut, into total silence. Hoods were placed over the heads of the victims. The hands were held behind their backs, and strung tight with plastic ties around the wrists. The contents of the Taurus were transferred into the Volkswagen, then the Ford's doors were closed and locked. This gave Hassan some hope, that Farhad's automobile may not be stripped of contents, whether inside or under the hood. Should they survive and return, they would escape in their Ford. Hassan could not figure out why they were kidnapped. There was nothing lucrative about apparently poor occupants of an old car. More puzzling, why they locked the doors of this aging automobile from intruders. Perhaps they had wised up to the fact, that the wealthy were now hiding their new cars, then driving in old autos, Hassan calculated.

One gunman jumped into the driver's seat, while the other man sat in the back of the Volkswagen. He pointed his gun at the two bound- and-gagged victims, who lay on the VW's floor.

After some turns and twists, Sami and Hassan felt a stretch of straight highway driving. The setting sun shone directly into the eyes of the driver, who occasionally swerved, when temporarily blinded by light. Complaining to the rear gunman about the sun, the driver inadvertently conveyed to Sami and Hassan that the VW was driving westward from Baghdad. The long stretch of driving told the desperate two, on the van's floor, that they were heading for Fallujah, if not Ramadi--both violent Sunni cities, at the time. Though Sunni himself, Hassan thought his Shiite name might doom him, before the kidnappers would give him a chance to explain, how a Sunni could possibly bear a Shiite name. They never bothered to learn about Sunni Kurds and their customs. It was no use lecturing them, that many of their famous and revered Sunnis had Shiite names.

Chapter 34--Kidnapped to Fallujah

STILL BLINDFOLDED, SAMI AND Hassan felt that the kidnappers' VW van slowing down, followed by various turns. From the driving time, Sami estimated they were in Fallujah. The Volkswagen stopped, and the hooded victims were pulled out of the van, dragged into a house and dumped on the floor of some room. Hassan scraped an elbow, while Sami bruised a rib. The door was locked, leaving the two alone by themselves. Not being able to see any furniture, they just sat on the floor, in the lotus position. When alone, Hassan whispered that Sami not give his sick dad's phone or address to the kidnappers, in any ransom negotiations, no matter what. Furthermore, he worried, that a phone call from the kidnappers could kill his father. If not, a visit by them at Baba's disclosed address, would definitely finish him off. Instead, Hassan thought that Sami should give them Farhad's telephone, pretending he was Sami's uncle. Zakho was too far away, for any outlaws to harm Farhad. Their only option would be to negotiate by phone.

"That's unfair to Farhad, without even consulting with him," Sami whispered back, turning his hooded face towards Hassan.

"How can we consult, with him in the mountains of Kurdistan? Just don't worry. I'll explain to Farhad, and take the blame, if ever we survive this." Hassan was barely audible.

Muffled voices seeped through the door, from an adjacent room. Sami faintly heard the words 'five hundred dollars', and little else. Soon the door opened. Sami and Hassan were ordered out, then pushed into a pickup truck, with their belongings thrown after them. The new vehicle's floor smelled of urine and motor oil. A canvas was pulled over them, covering the truck's cargo section. It was then tied down to side hooks, drastically reducing air circulation. The accumulating odors were becoming unbearable under the canvas. The truck driver was quickly off, on a much shorter drive, to a likely second Fallujah safe house. Still hooded, with hands tied, Hassan and Sami were unloaded from the pickup truck and shoved onto a floor. They sat up, crossed legged, on a throw rug. Hassan constantly invoked the name of Allah. Being a devout Muslim, he accepted his fate as the will of God; that worrying would not change one word of his scripted life. Sami, secular till now, prayed hard, just in case there was God up there, ready to help him out of this mental and emotional foxhole. To him, it was more like an American-style insurance policy.

The two prisoners heard a phone ring. Then, a faint conversation wafted into the locked room, followed by a distant thud of a dropped receiver. It rang again, a few minutes later, with more muffled words seeping through the door cracks, to reach Sami and Hassan. Again the phone was hung up, and the weak, distant voice stopped. This routine went on for over an hour.

Without warning, the deadbolt clicked loudly, and the door quickly swung open, onto the two desperate, hooded human beings, sitting on their haunches. The crime of these innocent souls, was being in the wrong place at the wrong time. In this Iraqi roulette, the loaded chamber finally caught up, dragging them relentlessly into a sectarian black hole. Two bearded men in disdasha dresses, stepped inside. From behind the hood, Sami and Hassan could only see, on the floor, open-toed slippers, with the large dirty toe in a separate sandal compartment. Each pulled one victim by the arm, and forcefully lead them back to the stinky bed of the same pickup truck of their last short trip. Sami was limping, as Hassan shed a tear. During the fifteen-minute journey, with their mouth-tape loosened, they managed a little whispering conversation.

"Why all these stops?" Hassan asked the expert on Baghdad. Sami thought the first group specialized in initiating kidnappings, like grabbing them off the street.

"We were then sold for five hundred dollars to a second gang, probably middlemen for a third bunch, who don't venture outside. They specialize in extracting ransom, in ways I don't want to think about right now." Sami's shaking voice faded away, as the truck pulled into the open garage of a house. Waiting was a man wearing kaffiyeh and sandals. He quickly closed the garage door, then rushed to the street. He confirmed that no one was following the truck.

Inside the house, Sami and Hassan were led to a small end room. A floor board was lifted and the lead guard, waving an AK-47 rifle stepped down. The rear henchman followed the docile victims with a menacing PKC Russian machine gun, which poked Sami's back. He, in turn, was following Hassan, down a short flight of stairs. The front man was pulling him in a rough manner. It was clear from the voice and demeanor of their hosts, that these were the new jailors, whose boss held their fate in a bloodied iron fist. Sami was visibly shaking, but Hassan, being a religious fatalist, was much calmer. The Quran had revealed that his life followed a pre-destined plan. No creature of Allah could alter His preordained path, from birth to death.

Chapter 35--Scary Interrogations

THE LEADING WATCHMAN USHERED Sami and Hassan to one of two rooms. He then hopscotched down a long flight of stairs, into a cellar. The trailing guard slipped on a mask. Quickly, he pulled off the captives' hoods, opened the door, and pushed his helpless prisoners into the selected room. Throwing two slips of paper and a pen at them, he ordered each one to write his address and phone number. The guard locked the deadbolt on the peep-holed door, then left. The air in the small room felt like prior guests had emptied their bladders there. Also, reddish spots dotted the floor. To Hassan, they were remnants of scrubbed-off human blood. Keeping it to himself, he did not want to further exacerbate Sami's mental condition. Once again, he impressed on Sami, not to give them the address of Baba, who may not survive his illness at the shock of his kidnapped son. Both would give the same address of Zakho, in the province of Dahuk, as confirmed by the Ford's license plate. Hassan paused, waiting for Sami's approval. Nodding his agreement, Hassan continued, until their two versions were synchronized.

Shortly after, there was a jingle of keys. A loud clang followed, and the door swept open onto an agitated Sami, and a calm, resigned Hassan. The masked guard grabbed the two pieces of paper, which had been left with Sami and Hassan. They were then lead down a long flight of stairs, to a spacious basement. It was partitioned into a dozen cubicles, separated by tall, raw plywood walls. The room dividers did not reach the ceiling, allowing for air circulation. Plywood lettering indicated Chinese or Korean manufacture. The two prisoners were flung into separate, non-adjoining cubicles. The doors were immediately shut and locked by the guard, who held the PKC machine gun. Shortly after, he came back with a grim-faced young man, holding a Kodak disposable camera. A photo of each one was snapped, in their separate cubicles. Sami and Hassan were left alone again, to languish in their small compartments. Tired, hungry, they now also needed to go to the bathroom. Time was heading towards midnight.

Early next morning, the masked guard with the machine gun showed up at Hassan's cell. He was accompanied by an assistant, who wore a grey dishdasha robe, open-toed sandals and a kaffiyeh covering his hair. The sidekick tied Hassan's hands behind his back, with plastic string. He then lead him out to join a line of half-dozen prisoners on their way to a small bathroom. Amongst them was Sami. At the door, one prisoner at a time, was untied, given a water ibreeq, an Iraqi spouted can, to wash their rear. This was the approved Islamic method of ablutions. Rubbing off with toilet paper was not commonly used by Iraqis. As each prisoner exited the bathroom, he was re-tied, then sent to the end of the line. Meanwhile, a new hostage would similarly enter the bathroom. This continued until every prisoner had relieved and washed himself. They were all now lead back to their individual cubicles. It was all done in eerie silence, except for the sound of CNN news, coming from upstairs.

Later, Hassan was summoned. With hood on, he was taken to the interrogation room, upstairs. A heavyset, turbaned, middle aged man sat cross-legged on a large cushion, counting beads on a string. Each bead signified a revered being such as Allah, Muhammad, and the founder of his particular Islamic sect. He counted the small stringed round marbles in the order of religious significance. Being Sunni, Caliph Ali would not count in his bead rotation. A young man in worn-out blue jeans held a whip in one hand and a dagger in the other.

"Shall we start, Sheikhna?" said the youth, addressing his boss as 'our sheikh'. He beckoned the young man over.

"Start easy, Omar," whispered Sheikhna, in his ear. Omar stepped closer to Hassan, and put his hand over his shoulder.

"Your Zakho information does not help us. We must have a Baghdad address, and a good telephone number," the interrogator's voice was stern. Hassan insisted he had no Baghdad address or phone, and planned to go sightseeing with his friend. They would later sleep in an obscure hotel called Jaro, near Haidar Khana mosque. In fact there was no such room-rental establishment. Hassan remembered the old Jaro hotel in Zakho, and threw it into the conversation. There was no updated phone directory to verify a sojourner's shelter.

"Call that our local address and phone number," Hassan's voice reverberated from inside the hood.

"People are running away from Baghdad, and you've come for sightseeing. You're either crazy or lying. We know you're not crazy," Omar scratched Hassan's back with the dagger's tip, drawing a blood-red line. Suffering in silence, Hassan tried to keep his promise to Sami, about leaving his father's address and phone number out of their unholy murderous hands.

"The other big lie is that you are a Sunni! the whole world knows that Hassan is a Shiite name." Omar scratched another reddish dagger line on his flesh. Hassan insisted that Kurdish Sunnis did not discriminate between Shiite or Sunni names. Sheikhna nodded negatively to Omar. In that Baghdad mayhem, Hassan figured it was impossible to persuade sectarian fanatics. To them, a Sunni, anywhere, could not possibly bear a Shiite name. Sheikhna pointed at Hassan, then moved his finger towards Omar. This signified a respite from interrogation, as well as a stern warning. Omar then gave Hassan just one day to provide local information, or he would not see the light of day again. Opening the door, the outside guard escorted Hassan to his tiny living space. Waiting for the next victim, Sheikhna flipped through prisoner photos, reading the short blurbs at the bottom. He then turned on a corner television set to CNN.

Chapter 36--Discovering a New Hero

THE NEXT HOSTAGE TO be grilled was Sami. By now, he was jumpy and psychologically debilitated, as they hauled him for questioning, in what was labeled as the confession room. After a light knock, the door opened into the interrogation room, with Sheikhna regally seated. His cheek twitched, signifying nervous impatience. Sami was hurled onto the hard marble floor, and hit on the head with a dagger's handle, then kicked. Sheikhna nodded approval.

"The documents we dug out of your car say you are an American pilot and an Iraqi traitor. Tell us why we should not behead you right now!" Omar struck Sami with his whip. Sheikhna told Omar to hold off a minute, as he raised the TV volume. It was about the Pope's assassination. A global search was on for a definite suspect--American Air Force colonel Sami Yusuf. His picture occupied the whole screen. Sheikhna examined Sami's photo,which he had pulled out of his victims' album. He compared it to the television undated image. There was a definite resemblance, and he was dumbfounded.

"Did you really kill the crusade leader, that son-of-a-dog, the papa?" Sheikhna asked, in a friendly voice. Papa being the Arabic name for pope. Sami's hooded head shook in agreement.

Sheikhna waved Omar out of the room, closing the door behind. He walked over to Sami, gently removed his hood, cut his plastic handcuff, then told the shaking Sami to rise. Sami stood up, looking down at his shoes. Sheikhna hugged Sami and kissed him twice on each cheek.

"You slew the enemy of Islam. Sit down, dear brother, and tell me how you did it, in your own holy words; not the way imperialist Christians are wailing about it," said Sheikhna to an astonished Sami. he was not sure how to react. Nevertheless, this was his ticket out of here. Sami told his story, minus the real motivation: the unforgivable violation by a Christian, penetrating the rectum of a Muslim. For that shame and loss of honor, Sami would have been immediately beheaded. But only Sami and his Christian lover, Luke, in San Francisco, knew what the late Pope, as Jesuit Father Rogan, had done to Sami. He could not reveal studying at Baghdad Jesuit highschool, instead of an Islamic madrasa. At the end of Sami's story, Sheikhna was even more impressed. He rose and kissed Sami again on the cheeks, and asked him if he was hungry or wished for anything.

A little more confident, Sami asked that Hassan be released and reunited with Farhad's old Ford, so Sami could visit his sick father. Sheikhna told Omar to bring Hassan over; but he advised Sami not to go see his father now. The place would be under round-the-clock police watch, waiting for him. Also, he would transfer Sami to the care of another person, who could protect him better, and would ensure a safe visit to his father. Sheikhna, of course, did not reveal his private business deal with this new party, nor Sami's monetary worth in this deal.

Soon, Omar walked in with Hassan, who was still hooded and hand-tied. Sheikhna beckoned to Sami. He got up, untied Hassan's hands, then removed the hood, then smiled at Hassan's visible face. Puzzled, Hassan figured Sami had gone over the edge, and lost his mind for sure.

"Sit down, you're amongst friends," said Sheikhna, offering him a cigarette and a chai istikan, Iraqi cup of tea. Hassan was all confused at this incredible reversal of fortunes. Sheikhna explained he'd just found out, that his friend, Sami, was an Islamic hero for killing crusaders' king, the hated Pope. Hassan relaxed, as his glum face evolved into confidence. Now he saw Sami as a savior.

Sheikhna told Omar to bring more tea istikans for his guests. Omar obliged, and looked apologetically at Sami, who still appeared tired. Picking up the cellphones from the coffee table, Sheikhna stared at it a few seconds, then dropped it back.

"They can listen in on this phone. Get me the house phone, with the long cord," he ordered Omar, who instantly complied. With the phone in, he pressed the door against the phone cord and shut it. Sheikhna eagerly dialed, on the secure line.

"Abu Jabbar, salam alaikum. I bring you joyous news for all Muslims--Allahu akbar. Our brother, Sami Yusuf, is my guest here. He's the one who fatally vanquished the Vatican crusader, silencing forever that son-of-a-dog anti-Islamic Pope. I'm serious! Have I ever joked on such matters?! Yes, yes he's the exact same one on CNN. Why don't you believe me? Alright, come here and meet him in person. We can also discuss the details of brother Sami becoming your honored guest," Sheikhna hung up, with a proud smirk on his face. His forefinger vigorously pulled each one of the stringed beads, to coincide with Allah, Muhammad, and others on his moving lips.

Chapter 37--The Transfer

A BLACK TOYOTA WAGON, with dark tinted windows arrived, and drove into Sheikhna's open garage. The waiting Omar immediately closed the garage door. A young, handsome man emerged from the car. Of average height and build, he wore a dishdasha, with a checkered kaffiyeh covering his head. He had a small beard and moustache. Omar lead him to a special private room, then informed Sheikhna of Abu Jabbar's arrival.

In a jiffy, Sheikhna was there, ordering Omar to fetch tea and the best of their mezze, the local name for appetizers. He offered Abu Jabbar shish kebab and Aleppo kubba, from a nearby restaurant, famous for Iraqi cuisine. Having already had a meal, Abu Jabbar settled just for mezze snacks. Omar was soon back, with several little plates of attractive delicacies, as well as a large teapot, and istikans. Sheikhna beckoned Omar to stand outside, to ensure that no one listened in, or disturbed their private discussions.

Alone in the room, Sheikhna and Abu Jabbar sat back, then exchanged the traditional Iraqi greeting, Allah belkhair, meaning God's blessing. First, they traded family news, Iraqi style, before settling down to business. Even then, serious negotiations had to await Abu Jabbar's confirmation of his ultimate catch: a truly grand prize for him, judging from his body language. In other words, he had to see for himself, that vaunted Sami, in person. Sheikhna called Omar to summon Sami. Soon, he was at the door--timid and apprehensive. Abu Jabbar received him with a warm smile, ushering Sami to a comfortable seat, near his leather chair. He now felt at ease. With no time to waste, Abu Jabbar started his probing, but friendly, questioning of Sami. He wanted to verify that he was the real pope killer, despite being pursued by Italy and the West. Sami's replies checked out with Abu Jabbar's information. He kept his facts in a small, green-covered notebook, that he had pulled out of his breast pocket. Eyeing Sheikhna, Abu Jabbar nodded approval. Sami was whisked back to his new comfortable room. The two then discussed Sami's worth, and set a price on this rare find: a real pope slayer.

"We would like to purchase Sami from you. Al Qaeda has authorized me to offer you one hundred thousand dollars cash for him," said Abu Jabbar.

"You are our dear brother, and Al Qaeda is important in the struggle against the crusaders and infidels. They are offering five million dollars for brother Sami. Could you not at least match the Great Satan?" pleaded Sheikhna. He put on the airs of a good Muslim, rather than a money-grabbing kidnapper. Abu Jabbar explained that Al Qaeda could get him one million dollars, but it will take time. Was he not aware of all the obstacles the imperialist Americans have put on international money movement? The slow hawala-type of money order and cash money movement had replaced the instant electronic transfer, Abbu Jabbar explained. That he could give Sheikhna a hundred thousand in cash now. The rest he could get within two months.

"Your word is as good as gold to me, brother Abu Jabbar. But we have immediate obligations to pay people who may bring us godless blasphemers at any time, for cash on the spot. Could you not help us with the balance within one month?" asked Sheikhna.

Abu Jabbar responded, that he would get the money soon, inshallah, God willing, and handed him a large envelope. Glancing inside, Sheikhna counted a hundred bundles of thousand-dollar bills.

"Shukran, brother Abu Jabbar," Sheikhna thanked him, pleased with the sight of all that cash on hand-- more than any he had ever seen before. "Then it's agreed. I will have the rest within one month, inshallah. Your word is as good as Holy Quran's truths." Sheikhna put the envelope in a wall safe, locked it, and re-covered the safe's door with the framed Quranic quote: all Muslims are brothers. He then unlocked the room's entrance door, and told Omar to fetch their honored Pope killer. Sami Yusuf was now the new Al Qaeda high-value prize. As soon as Sami appeared, Abu Jabbar rushed to greet him, kissing him on the two cheeks several times, then offered his comfortable seat. Sami smiled politely, still unable to make heads or tails of the whole situation.

"You have done to the arch crusader what we, at Al Qaeda, have been dreaming of doing for a long time, my dearest brother, Sami," said Abu Jabbar. Sami moved in his chair, trying to put on a smile. He was not sure if his bad luck would return, just as quickly. "Sheikhna has agreed that we can provide you better protection from the Global Satan and the Vatican infidels. They want to catch and hang you, for doing the Muslims the greatest deed since Salahudeen, of the Ayyubite dynasty, kicked the crusaders out of Jerusalem. The infidels still remember him as

Saladin the Great." Abu Jabbar felt a kinship to Saladin. He had the same ultimate goal of liberating Jerusalem and returning Dome of the Rock, the third holiest Muslim shrine, to Islamic control. Not able to match the rhetoric, Sami just kept saying "shukran", which was Iraqi for "thank you", forcing one smile after another. "You are now the honored guest of Al Qaeda of Iraq. Being their leader here, I'm responsible for your safety and security," Abu Jabbar rose and kissed Sami on the cheeks again, as Sami just uttered "shukran", sheepishly.

As everyone got ready to transfer Sami to Abu Jabbar's protective custody, Sami wanted to know what would happen to Hassan.

"Your friend, dear brother Sami, is our precious friend too," said Abu Jabbar. "We can see that he gets back to Kurdistan safely, in the car he came in. Or we can arrange transportation, through our secure channels." Abu Jabbar, for a moment, looked like Aladdin's genie to Sami, offering him a wish or two.

Chapter 38--Al-Qaeda's Honored Guest

SAMI ASKED HIS CAPTOR-TURNED-HOST for a private meeting with Hassan, to find out his real needs. The door opened onto Hassan, in the other room. Sami walked in, as Omar closed the door behind them. They pretended to talk loud on harmless matters, but whispered as to intentions. Sami wanted Farhad's car to stay with Hassan, in case they had to make a dash for it, from Al Qaeda, American agents or Iraqi police. Hassan, who kept a spare car key in a secret pocket, had no objection. Sami then opened the door, and conveyed their desire about the old Ford, to the new host. Abu Jabbar was eager to please his prized possession, and did not worry about losing him. He was sure that Sami and his friend could not go anywhere, without Al Qaeda's protective network.

With no further delay, they all were ushered into Abu Jabbar's car, heading for another Fallujah location. Farhad's wagon followed, driven by an experienced cop-dodging operative. Arriving at a large warehouse, a waiting armed guard, with a cellphone, opened a large door. He let Abu Jabbar's car in, then quickly closed the gate. The warehouse was full of cars, vans and a Humvee, in various stages of outfitted high-powered chemicals, being readied for giant blasts. Farhad's car was parked in a hidden space outside the warehouse, away from informers, or eyes, prying for the authorities. The guard saluted, opening Abu Jabbar's car door. He then rushed ahead of him to clear the entrance into the house, where Abu Jabbar was currently headquartered. He beckoned the guard, to show his guests to their quarters.

It was more like a newsroom, a horror museum and a photo studio, all rolled into one. The walls were totally covered with pictures and press clippings of murders and tragedies, marked as Al Qaeda achievements. There were photos of the collapsing New York Twin Towers, colored pictures of Muhammad Atta, news clippings of the U.S. embassy bombings in Africa, the Cole explosion in Yemen. There were also the latest reports on the Pope's killing by Abu Jabbar's honored guest, Sami. Even the abandoned airplane, near Zakho, was squeezed in a corner of the crowded wall. In a rare moment of excitement, Sami pointed at the plane, for Hassan.

To Sami, it all looked bizarre. The restoration of his personal honor, by killing the Pope, was so badly misinterpreted. It qualified him to join a vile organization that indiscriminately bombed women, children and old men. This wasn't even collateral damage. Their plain murder repulsed Sami, being a killer of a different genre. But the show for survival had to go on, he figured. Besides, he had no choice but to cooperate, until his moment of escape was on hand. That included a photo and video session, the following day. Abu Jabbar had told Sami about it, during the car trip to the new location.

A young man in a blue cap and jeans hauled in a bed, folded onto a mattress and a pillow. It opened up into a comfortable bed.

"This for master Sami," said the help. He then left to fetch Hassan's bed, which was smaller, and had a stained mattress. The servant also left a white dishdasha-style night robe for Sami, and a black one for Hassan. The two immediately undressed and got into their respective Iraqi male night dresses, then slipped into the portable beds. They instantly fell asleep, after that long exhausting day.

Next morning at nine, there was a knock on the door, which then opened wide. A large brass circular tray was carried in by a woman, who was well covered, with a green scarf on her head. She placed the tray on a table then left, without a word. It was crammed with food that Sami and Hassan had not seen since they left Zakho. There was omelet of basterma, which was a uniquely-spiced Iraqi meat. Next to it was geymar, a breakfast delicacy made from thick moose cream; not to mention yogurt, local cheese, and hot summoon, the famous Baghdad oval bread. There was also a large pot of tea and two istikans, as well as a hot-water bowl and two cloths for subsequent wash-up, in the Iraqi tradition. The two wolfed everything down. They were dying for some good food. Also, a convenient Iraqi custom was, that eating it all, was a compliment to the host. Whereas leftovers meant the food was of low quality, which the host could take umbrage at. A handy toilet was close by. After relieving themselves, each one washed his rear with a spouted copper container, called ibreeq. It was the Iraqi way of cleaning, without toilet paper. Soon their cots had gone, and the room had reverted to a propaganda studio.

165

They then dressed up and sat ready. They did not want to get caught off guard, for whatever surprises that were planned for them. It was not long in coming. There was a knock on the door, and Abu Jabbar walked in, introducing an accompanying cameraman, as Mussawarchi, which was Iraqi for photographer. He then warmly greeted Sami, and profusely dished out compliments, while the camera was rolling. Abu Jabbar also informally greeted Hassan, who was not in the video. There was a respite from pictures. Abu Jabbar and his video maker explained to Sami, how he could help in making this news film a bomb shell, when broadcast over Al Jazeera TV. The initial impromptu mini-video was for Abu Jabbar's personal collection, they explained.

Mussawarchi gently moved Sami against the wall, near enlarged magazine clippings about the Pope's assassination. The pictures were sharp and clear, forming an excellent background for Abu Jabbar's photos. The photographer then asked Abu Jabbar to stand near Sami, without blocking the selected photos on the wall, behind them. The camera started, as Abu Jabbar asked Sami to explain how he killed Pope Urban IX. He pointed at the photos and clippings that covered the background wall. There were also personal close-ups, though more of Abu Jabbar than Sami. When the video session was over, Sami asked Abu Jabbar for a private word, on the side. He requested that the video's release be delayed, until after he saw his ill father. This, so his condition would not worsen, worrying about his fugitive son. Also, it would delay the authorities going in hot pursuit of him, until he saw his dad. It was agreed.

Abu Jabbar then quickly sat down with his security people, as well as Sami, about arranging for Sami to visit his father. Right after that, they would dispatch the video to Al Jazeera

TV station. They concurred that Hassan, who was not a wanted felon, would take Farhad's car to the house of Sami's dad. There, Baba would ride the car to Al-Rasheed hotel. It was a safe, secret rendezvous for Sami and his dad, near familiar Yafa street. Prior to that family reunion, a room would be reserved in Hassan's name at the hotel. It was also decided to paint the Ford black and tag it with Baghdad license plates. However, the painting had to be done inside Abu Jabbar's warehouse. It was almost full of wired vehicles, ready to blow up at pre-selected city spots. They could clear a space for one more car.

Chapter 39--The Suicide Plan

A FRESH NEW PROPOSAL Abu Jabbar wanted to sound Sami about, privately in his office. He explained to Sami, that the captured US Humvee, in the warehouse was being prepared for the visit of the US president, whose movements were top secret. But Al Qaeda had a mole inside Iraq's defense ministry. He would supply inside information, as to when the president was to arrive, along with his itinerary. There would be a half-dozen Humvees in the convoy, with US military personnel driving them. Abu Jabbar then stared into Sami's eyes.

"You have a choice of being a perennial fugitive, or captured and executed by the US. Or you can be an Iraqi, Arab and Islamic martyr, going straight to Heaven, with honey rivers and virgin houris awaiting you," said Abu Jabbar. Astonished, Sami asked what he had in mind for him. "Your military ID is very valuable, to sneak the explosive Humvee into the presidential convoy." Abu Jabbar pulled out Sami's identification card from his pocket, and handed it to Sami.

"But they all know me, from the Pope's killing, and my pictures and name on TV." Sami was surprised at this lapse of judgment.

"That's true, but look at your card carefully," said Abu Jabbar. Sami did notice the photo had been professionally altered, so he would not be easily recognized, in these fast, hectic times. Also, his name was slightly adjusted, with the 'Yu' in Yusuf blanked out, and an 'i' added in the end, to make his name "Sufi", delicately capitalizing the 's', utilizing their expert forgers.

All Sami could think of was seeing Baba. Then he would hire the best lawyer money could buy, to get out of a death sentence. The most lenient verdict he could hope for would be life imprisonment, unless he was able to manufacture some mitigating circumstances. Still, Sami saw dollar signs on Abu Jabbar's eyeballs, representing those five million the US had placed on the head of this Al Qaeda leader. That would make the best attorney happy to represent him, Sami figured. What about mitigating circumstances? He kept rubbing his forehead, searching for that magic idea that could save him. To Abu Jabbar, Sami was deciding to be the ultimate suicide bomber, ready to blast his prized catch, the President of the United States. He seemed ecstatic at the thought of a twin-kill, in one month, of the worst enemies of Islam: the Pope, and the US president.

"Alright, I'll do it, but Baba must not know; it will finish him off, way before his illness does it. When can I see him?" Sami looked enigmatic. Abu Jabbar assumed it was for all the unexpected surprises he would encounter in paradise. Sami also requested that the original Kurdistan license plates of Farhad's automobile be given to Hassan, in case he needed them, on his way back to Zakho. Like the last wish of a condemned man, it was granted. Right then the muezzin called for noon prayers. Sami excused himself, to go pray with Hassan, even though Sami had not prayed in years. As a believable martyr, he had to, now. More importantly, he wanted to discuss crucial matters with Hassan, in private, while Abu Jabbar was busy praying.

The little hallway between the two rooms had a small window. Peering through it, on the way to Hassan, he could see the Euphrates river flowing from his right to left, giving him general north-south bearings. Crossing the river, just south of him was a newer bridge, compared to an older one, several blocks north of him. The new bridge lead eastward to a busy road that he assumed was Highway 10, which he had heard Abu Jabbar's people talk about. Sami figured that the house was in the block, nearest the corner of Highway 10 and the new bridge.

The conversation with Hassan consisted of loud prayer talk, intertwined with whispers about Sami's intentions. He briefed Hassan on two plans: Abu Jabbar's martyrdom plan, and his own plan of preventing a presidential assassination. After that, how the two would make their way back to Zakho. Much depended on Sami finding someone in Al-Rasheed hotel to safely tip off, and thus foil Al Qaeda's plot. The hotel was popular with important foreign personnel. Hassan had grave reservations about the whole thing, but he had no choice but to go along with it. They were between Iraq and a hard place; that is, Al Qaeda and the US justice system. Abu Jabbar let Sami and Hassan arrange the meeting with Sami's father, in freedom, convinced that Sami would not trade Al Qaeda's protection, for capture and execution by the Yanks. The visit to Sami's parents had to start today, Thursday, and end the following day, the Muslim Sabbath of Friday. After the family reunion, but no later than Saturday, Sami was to report back to Abu Jabbar, to prepare for a momentous event, on Sunday. That would be the day of the presidential visit, Sami surmised.

There were some loose ends that had slipped everyone's mind. Hassan was to bring Baba, the senior Yusuf, to Al-Rasheed hotel, fulfilling Sami's lifetime goal of seeing his dad, with honor. Yet, Baba had no idea where Sami was, nor who on Earth Hassan might be. So, Sami sat down and composed a letter, to his father, in his familiar handwriting, for Hassan to deliver. In the letter, he urged his dad to follow Hassan's instructions exactly, as the only way they could finally meet. At the same time, Sami hoped and prayed, that his father would be well enough, to make it to the hotel. It was crucial for Baba to believe, that the plan was genuine, and not a journalistic plot, to secure an interview with the father of the Pope's killer. For extra authentication, Sami tore off the front page of that day's Baghdad newspaper, signed under the date, in Arabic, folded the page and inserted it into the envelope, along with his letter. Thus, there would be no doubt, as to when the letter was written, emphasizing the genuineness and immediacy of the matter. Sami's mother needed no proof of anything. She always gave him the benefit of the doubt.

"If that is not enough, throw in a family secret: they call me 'Simsim', for sesame in English; I don't know what you call it in Kurdish," said Sami.

"Kunji," interjected Hassan.

"That's a cute nickname too," replied Sami.

" Why did they call you that?" Hassan wondered.

Sami explained that at birth, he was so little, the midwife called Baba to come see 'Simsim'.

"Compared to rice, which is a daily staple, that's pretty small size. So the name stuck," Sami was getting nostalgic.

Hassan was not sure how to address Sami's parents. It was an Iraqi custom to address a married woman as mother, or um, of her oldest son. Also, a man would be addressed as father, or abu, of his oldest son.

"When I meet your mother, do I greet her as 'Um Sami'?" Hassan needed to know.

"Yes; I'm the oldest son," said Sami.

"Fine; that would then make your father 'Abu Sami'." Hassan was glad to learn of the informal, friendly appellation. Now he would not be seen as a total stranger, when visiting them, by himself.

Chapter 40--Logistics of a Meeting

IT WAS WARM, SUNNY and a little windy, on this Thursday afternoon of April, as Hassan drove Farhad's wagon out of Abu Jabbar's Fallujah garage. It's now repainted black, with Baghdad license plates. In front, sat Sami; behind them was an Al Qaeda soldier, guiding them onto Highway 10, to Baghdad. He was armed, but did not point the gun at anyone. His boss had instructed him, that Sami and Hassan were his guests. Nor were they flight risks. Sami desperately needed their protection, to avoid capture, prosecution and likely execution by the US, for assassinating the Pope. The henchman got off at a colleague's house, near the highway. Sami made mental notes of the directions, taken from Abu Jabbar's house, to the Baghdad freeway. He was careful not to arouse suspicion. When alone, and safely on the way, Sami wrote his information on a piece of paper, as best as he could remember. He then folded and tucked it in his pocket. The sky was brown, from a dust storm, that stayed with them, till shortly before arriving at Iraq's capital. First stop in Baghdad, was Al-Rasheed hotel. Hassan checked into the room, being reserved in his name. Sami waited in the car. Then, with the help of a couple of bribes, Hassan smuggled him into the room, to await his parents. Meanwhile, Hassan drove off to the Mansur district, to fetch Baba and Mama. Sami, now with earned pride, could finally see, touch and feel the dearest two persons in his life. It had been a terribly long absence.

The now-black Ford turned left into the alleyway, between the home of Yusuf, Sr. and the neighbor's house. Hassan got out, gave a cautionary glance around, then walked to the elder Yusufs' entrance door. A rotund woman, in black dress and head scarf, opened the door. She looked sad and suspicious.

"Um Sami?" Hassan glanced at the envelope in his hand. She nodded in the affirmative.

"Khair, blessed, be the news. Abu Sami is in fine health, inshallah, God willing?" asked Hassan, looking at her mourning outfit.

"He is well, Allah be praised. Who may you be?" Mrs. Yusuf's curiosity piqued some more.

"My name is Hassan," he said. Gasping at the Shiite name, she turned to close the front door.

"I'm a Kurdish friend of Simsim," he quickly added, and handed her the letter from her son. At the sound of her son's nickname, she re-opened the door. Also, she knew that Kurds were Sunni, like her. Mrs. Yusuf relaxed and invited Hassan in, seating him in her best soft leather chair. She then rushed upstairs to show the letter to her husband. Hassan could hear 'Simsim' repeated, and sounds of subdued jubilation, with some female sobbing. A tear rolled down Hassan's cheek. She reappeared at the top of the stairs.

"Hassan, my eye, when can we go see Sami?" Mrs. Yusuf was wiping her face with a black kerchief.

"Khalla, auntie, anytime you are ready, I am," Hassan stood up, in respect. He added that it would be advisable to leave Farhad's Ford in their closed garage, and go by taxi to the Al-Rasheed hotel. Having lived in sectarian fear, any added precaution was fine with her.

"Abu Sami will be ready soon. He'll need your help to aid him down the stairs," Mrs. Yusuf said. Showing great deference, Hassan asked to let him know when to come upstairs. She asked him to fetch the wheelchair from a backroom closet, then come up.

In the bedroom, Hassan saw a tall, once-handsome man, weakened by illness. He was getting on his feet from the bed, with his wife's help. Hassan hurried to lend a hand. The senior Yusuf had a moustache and a beard, though he had been clean-shaven, in all the photos that Sami had shown Hassan. The elder Yusuf apologized for his hairy appearance. Mrs Yusuf interrupted to explain, that since their barber was murdered by bearded religious fanatics, he stopped going to the barbershop. He did not dare shave at home, either.

After a long, anxious wait, the cab arrived. Traffic had been diverted, because of a suicide bombing, according to the cabdriver. Mrs. Yusuf recited lines from the Kursi chapter of the Quran, then puffed air at her husband, signifying the blowing away of Satan and his evil from him. While Hassan helped the senior Yusuf to the back of the car, the wife put on a black abaya over her outfit, covering her from the neck down. A black, see-through pushiyya veiled her face. Hassan politely helped her into the second back seat, next to her husband. Quickly taking his seat in front, Hassan signaled the taxi driver to proceed carefully.

On their way to the hotel, they passed by a demolished vehicle, surrounded by several devastated shops, as well as other cars. A woman in black sat crying on a bench. Everyone was silent for a spell. The taxi stopped at the closest point, that security personnel allowed. Hassan got out and opened the door for Mrs. Yusuf. Then they both pulled out the collapsed wheelchair, and unfolded it for the senior Yusuf. Attempting to pay the cabdriver, Hassan was emphatically overruled by Mrs. Yusuf, handing the taxi operator the full fare and a generous baqsheesh tip, on top of that. Promptly, they proceeded towards the hotel, with Hassan wheeling Sami's father.

Chapter 41--The Reunion

IT WAS EXTRA BUSY that night, at Al-Rasheed hotel, judging from the number of people milling around, and the weary hotel employees, hurrying and scurrying. In addition to being the eve of the Muslim Sabbath, Friday, there apparently were also a lot of foreign guests staying there. A linguistic and sartorial evaluation indicated that most of them were US military and civilian personnel, on some kind of important mission, like perhaps laying the groundwork for a VIP visit from America. Acting confident, like he belonged there, Hassan pushed the elder-Yusuf's wheelchair, alongside the veiled Mrs. Yusuf, to Hassan's reserved room, where America's most wanted man was waiting for his parents.

At the hotel room, Hassan knocked, as a courtesy, then quickly opened the door, with a spare key, saving Sami a risky appearance at the entrance. Mrs. Yusuf flipped the pushiyya veil back, over her head, revealing her face, as Hassan ushered Sami's Baba and Mama into the room. He quickly took his leave, to fetch them dinner, and allow total privacy, during a highly-emotional family meeting. Hassan instantly closed the door behind, before any curious passerby could glance inside, and possibly identify the high-value guest.

Sami stood there incredulous, as to the reality of the moment, while Mama rushed to kiss and embrace her long-lost son, wiping her wet eyes, as best as she could.

"Simsim, Simsim! My heart, my life, I did not believe I'd see my dear son again!" she sobbed, as Sami lead her to a comfortable chair, and handed her a hotel Kleenex box. He then walked over to Baba, still in the wheelchair, knelt down and kissed his hand, in the traditional Iraqi way of respecting their elders. Sami then hugged and kissed his dad. Afterwards, he helped him out of the wheelchair, onto an easy sofa, and sat beside him.

"You've lost weight, Simsim, my eyes. Don't they feed you good?" his mom removed her abaya and placed it beside her.

"Mama, no one can cook your dolma, kubba and kebab, so I can eat it all up," said Sami. Baba appeared pleased, and nodded in agreement. He then turned to his dad: "I know there's a smile somewhere on your face, Baba, but I can't see it, from all this beard and moustache," Sami laughed as did Baba and Mama.

"What can we do, Simsim. Our rulers used to kill bearded people. Now, bearded people kill beardless men!" his dad whispered. Mama explained, that all hotel rooms and many homes were bugged, during that. In time, everyone got used to whispering, all the time. Baba leaned over to Sami. "What's this about you and the Pope? Did you really kill him?" whispered Baba. Sami nodded assent, but quickly added, that it was not jihad against the crusaders, as the newsmen were repeating. Rather, it was a personal matter of honor. Sami's father was puzzled as to how the Pope could induce such a violent reaction.

"Baba, do you remember when you registered me at Baghdad Jesuit high?" Sami looked intently at his dad, who responded without hesitation, that the memory was still vivid. "Do you recall the priest, who showed you both the campus and the boarding house?" Sami added. "Don't know his name, Simsim. If you show me his picture of those years, I could point him out," said his dad.

"Well, that was Father Rogan, who became Pope Urban IX. It's his pictures that you see all over television--next to mine." Sami walked over and hugged his shocked mother. "Don't cry, Mama; I have a plan that will save me, and I can come back as a free man, for good," he dabbed her eyes with tissue. Baba beckoned Sami to sit next to him.

"Tell me, Simsim, what is it that Rogan or anyone else could do to you, which would deserve a death sentence from you?" Baba was baffled. "You always told me the truth," he added.

"Baba, the son-of-a-dog molested me," Sami looked down, "when I was young and naive, in his care at the Jesuit school." He covered his cheeks with his hands. "I couldn't face you again, until I restored our family honor." Sami would not elaborate on the unforgivable, perhaps to Baba, and non-cleansable honor of being violated in the anus, and by a Christian, to boot.

There was a knock on the door. Sami jumped to unlock and open it. He stayed behind the door, to keep out of sight of any corridor walkers. Hassan stepped in with hot kebabs, mezze snacks, hot summoon bread, and tea leaves, from the market. The hotel kitchen provided, thanks to a bribe, a teapot, istikan-type of teacups, and ceramic plates. With Hassan quickly inside, Sami shut and locked the door, then helped him set the table and brew the tea. The two aided Baba and Mama to the table, then Hassan left for an outside snack, giving them further privacy time.

The family talked old times, and avoided Simsim's personal matters, so as not to depress Mama. Concerned about expenses, Baba broached Simsim, about how his funds were holding up, in this trip. If he needed help, not to be too proud to ask him for it, in these perilous times. The son assured him, that he had adequate funds taped under the Ford, which was parked in their garage. Even if it were not so, Sami was not going to saddle his parents with any expenses, knowing that they could barely pay their way, these days.

After a while, Hassan returned. He advised, that it was too risky at night, for Sami's mother and father to travel home. He recommended that they wait for daylight. There were two king-size beds. The parents would occupy one and Sami the other. The parents hesitated, concerned about Hassan's accommodation. Sami assured them that Hassan had secured a separate nearby room, thanks to another bribe. Iraqi cultural mores and family honor dictated that, only close family members shared the same sleeping quarters.

Chapter 42--The Farewell

AT DAWN, THE MUEZZIN called the faithful to prayer, from a nearby mosque, judging by the minaret's powerful speakers. To all the Yusufs, it was like a radio alarm that went off too soon. They just wiggled in their beds, and continued their sleep. Religion, to them, was a private matter, between the person and God. Public prayer and collective Ramadan fasting was faith flaunting, to them, compared to their subdued style. Seeing themselves as good Muslims, they helped the poor and donated food to the clerical mullahs of their local mosque. When Baba was healthy, he used to take Simsim to the Friday sermon, if given by a logical, rather than a fanatical clergyman. He was anxious that Sami keep in touch with his roots, without exposure to religious zealots, with their strict fundamentalist interpretations of the Holy Quran. To expose Sami to other views and beliefs, his dad sent him to Baghdad Jesuit high. Their motto was 'we don't teach; we educate'. Unfortunately, that bold experiment veered into its own tragic twist, which was still unfolding. Those were secular times in Iraq. Sami remembered Baba asking a porter, at Haidar Khana mosque, near Mansur, questions about his beliefs and politics.

"Religion is for Allah, but Iraq is for us all," said the lowliest citizen of the day. Sami had not heard such profundity from any Iraqi leader, in decades.

In contrast to the Yusufs, Hassan got up, unrolled his personal rug and prayed, as he had always done, in Zakho and on trips. Faith had served him well in tough times. That God had scripted his life, provided a healthy fatalism. It often saved him a lot of anguish, when cornered by evil doers. He would just leave everything to God. He would just follow the path laid out for him by the Creator, without worrying about his decisions being right or wrong. Like most Kurds, Hassan was passionate about Kurdistan, but religiously, never fanatical enough to go blow up innocent women and children of rival sects or beliefs. He would recall, that at the height of the Baghdad's murder spree against the Kurds, his people never took it out on innocent Arab civilians. Even those, whom Baghdad's dictator brought in to settle on expropriated Kurdish homes and lands, were not harmed, despite being part of his Arabization policy. The government's grip on Kurdistan loosened, after a prior American intervention. Still, there were no Kurdish reprisals against the transplanted Arab civilians.

At around 10 a.m., Hassan visited the room of Sami and his parents, to see if they were ready for breakfast. Abu Sami gave Hassan directions to Ammu Ilyas Deli, on nearby Al-Rashid Street. Ammu, or Uncle in Iraqi, made the best basterma and egg omelet, Baba declared, to the consternation of Mama. She insisted that no one could beat her homemade basterma. Sami's mother described how she personally minced prime beef cuts, then added her own mix of herbs and hot spices. Then she would stuff the resulting basterma meat into sheep's intestines, stretched into flat paddles. The domestic help would subsequently hang the meat from outdoor clothes lines, to mature during the cold winter months. That provided natural refrigeration as well. Sami sided with Mama against Uncle Ilyas.

"Alright, since Mama's basterma is not available now, can we settle for second best?" said Baba. The opposition smiled and nodded their agreement. Hassan then stepped outside the room, and closed the door behind, on his way to the deli.

After breakfast, the Yusuf family spent some precious time together, till late afternoon. Mama and Baba would have to leave before Baghdad's darkness descended upon them. Prior to Hassan fetching a cab, to escort the elder Yusufs home, Sami had a private session with him, in Hassan's hotel room. There, Sami disclosed his plan to save himself from the US death penalty, and possibly end up with a light sentence. Should the scheme fail, Sami would find his way to dad's garage, and hide in Farhad's Ford. Hassan would then quickly take off for Zakho. Even Baba and Mama were not to know, thus sparing them police searches and legal problems. When checking out of his own hotel room, Hassan would pay for Sami's room till Sunday. Between now and Monday, Hassan would be the guest of the senior Yusufs, in Mansur. By Monday, Sami would hopefully sneak into the Taurus wagon, in Baba's garage. If not, they would likely hear about the whereabouts of Colonel Sami Yusuf, in the news. Either way, Hassan would drive home to Zakho, with or without Sami, no later than Tuesday morning."If I abandon you here, Farhad will never forgive me." Hassan was terribly upset. Sami begged him to understand that without his plan, America's global tentacles would pick him up, sooner or later. It would mean the death sentence, for using his US military position to assassinate a head of state, not to mention the leader of a billion Catholics.

In the other room, the elder Yusufs were ready to leave. Mama even covered her face with the pushiyya veil, waiting for Hassan to push Baba's wheelchair forward. Kneeling, Sami kissed his dad's hand, then rose to hug him. Mama lifted her black veil, for one final tearful hug, kissing her eldest son. With her pushiyya back on, the parents and Hassan were ready to depart for the taxi, and onto their Mansur home.

Chapter 43--Scheming Emissary

FRIDAY NIGHT AT AL-RASHEED hotel was lonely for Sami. He tossed and twisted in bed, till well past midnight. This physical activity exhausted him, and he fell into a deep sleep. At dawn, the muezzin's call to prayer, on loudspeakers, woke him up. Soon after, there was a knock on his door. Expecting a visit from Abu Jabbar's people, Sami opened the door, and stood behind it, out of sight of possible hotel patrons. In, walked a medium-built young man, carrying a rolled-up rug under the left arm, and a beaded string in his right hand. He wore local Iraqi garb, consisting of dishdasha dress, and kaffiyeh headgear. His well-worn sandals had a separate compartment each, for the dirty big toes. He instantly recognized Sami, from CNN, Al Jazeera, and front-page photos of every newspaper. After the traditional God-is-great greeting, he introduced himself as Mullah Ahmad.

"Looks like you did not have any trouble getting into the hotel, Mullah," Sami addressed him respectfully by his religious title, equivalent to reverend.

"My nephew works in the kitchen, nushkur Allah, thank God." He spread his prayer rug on the clean hotel carpet, in a north-south direction. For a prayer to be valid, the rug had to be very clean, and untouched by any animal. This is why pets were never popular in Islamic countries, Sami surmised. Mullah Ahmad slipped into the bathroom. He performed the ritualistic ablutions, in the tub, using the ibreeq, an Iraqi spouted container. Leaving the bathroom, he headed for his personal rug. Carefully stepping on it, he faced south, towards Mecca, and performed the required dawn prayer. Sami warily watched from the side of his eye. In the end, the mullah looked left, then right, cursing the devil away. After that, he grabbed his beads, and pulled them one by one. With each touched bead, he recited a holy Islamic name. He then asked Sami if he had done his mandatory prayers yet. Sami pretended that he meant to, but he forgot his rug in the car, which took his parents home. It was unclean, to pray on the hotel carpet, sullied by infidels, Sami added. The cleric immediately offered his own personal rug to pray on. It would be consecrated by the sacred martyr, Sami Yusuf, the brave slayer of the Pope, king of the crusaders.

Remembering how others had prayed in front of him, Sami went through the motions, as best as he could. Mullah Ahmad was too busy looking at some papers, which he had pulled out of his pocket and laid them out on the table. As soon as Sami was done, he rolled up the rug and politely handed it to the mullah. He rested it against the door, to remember taking it with him, on the way out. Moving back to the table, he asked Sami to join him, and go over tomorrow's plans. The radio was turned on loud, as per Abu Jabbar's instructions. Mullah Ahmad started the discussion, certain that the radio would drown out their words for any listener outside, or secret bug inside.

Beginning with a summary, the holy man explained that a prized personage was arriving from America. A well-placed agent had informed Al Qaeda leadership, that the visitor was likely to be the US president himself. Just before sunrise, the following day, Sunday, the VIP was scheduled to arrive from Jordan, in a commercial Fokker F-28 jet, instead of a conspicuous American plane. In Baghdad, the small jet would arrive at 30, 000 feet directly over the international airport, before plunging into a spiral dive, down to about a hundred feet above the runway. The Fokker would then straighten out and land, in the manner of most commercial jets that flew into Baghdad.

"We have a portable rocket, from the Afghan-Russian war," said the pious man, referring to a shoulder-fired Stinger missile, in Al Qaeda's possession. The only such missile was left behind by the Americans, following the Russian retreat from Afghanistan. Al Qaeda had saved it up, for the highest ranking American they could get, Mullah Ahmad explained, with a gleam in his eyes. It clearly foretold, that the historic moment was imminent. They had, in vain, tried to bring down airplanes, that have been landing at Baghdad International airport, using plain rockets. The target soared too high above the airport, before falling like a rock, past the cross-hairs of Al Qaeda's guns, the mullah explained, with animated gestures. Sami was getting edgy as he listened with feigned intensity.

"We have an Afghan veteran, who's ready to fire the Stinger, from a secure hide-out, near the airport. But, Al Qaeda planners think, that you can do the job much better. You must be very knowledgeable about US weaponry, being in their Air Force." Mullah Ahmad looked at him. Colonel Sami Yusuf immediately replied, that he had never carried a Stinger launcher, let alone shoot a missile out of it. The rockets he had used, were sophisticated missiles, sent off combat jets. One of those killed the king of the crusaders, in Rome, putting it in their jihadist jargon. Delighted, Mullah Ahmad rose with pride, and kissed Sami on both cheeks. He then drew Sami's attention to the papers on the table. They described plan B in detail, should plan A, the airport Stinger, fail to hit VIP's jet, while diving for a safe landing.

Chapter 44--Moving to the Site

THE MAIN MISSION OF Mullah Ahmad was to explain Plan B to Sami, in detail. Plan A was the Stinger missile attempt on the VIP's Fokker, while dive-landing at Baghdad International airport. He would then give their new martyr, Sami, a set of instructions, elaborate on them, and answer any questions, before the cleric could leave the hotel. To allay any fears of failure, the Al Qaeda emissary was instructed, to provide their suicide man, with any reassuring plot background, needed to bolster his morale. They had every confidence, that the Pope's killer could be trusted with any secret information. Besides, no one else would dare protect Sami from the Americans, who would surely execute him anyway. In short, there was not the slightest doubt, in the jihadists' minds, that Sami would prefer their martyrdom to a dishonorable American death.

A rolled spreadsheet, which came inside Mullah Ahmad's rug, was laid out over the table. The cleric pored over this clearly-illustrated local map, with Sami. The central part of it was the International airport, and the highway towards downtown Baghdad. Sami was curious about the x-mark. It was penciled in, at some distance from the airport, along the highway, towards the Green Zone. From this point, a line was drawn upwards, perpendicular to the airport road, going to a warehouse, that stored building materials, for a Talal Shakir. During the day, he was a contractor, who provided much of the cement barriers for government, and other office structures. After normal business hours, he helped insurgents and Al Qaeda get rid of foreign occupiers. At the highway's x-location, Sami would see two flags, explained the cleric: an Iraqi flag on one side of the road, and an American flag on the opposite side. That same 'x' also marked the end of a hidden tunnel, which Shakir had dug, starting from his warehouse. It took Talal three months of night work, to supervise the digging of the underground tube. A huge volume of dirt was transported, as legitimate material, to his legal construction sites. The tunnel's end-chamber, under the highway, brimmed with dynamite sticks, wired to be triggered, the moment Abu Jabbar's explosive Humvee drove above the chamber. That would simultaneously set off the Humvee, above, and the packed room, below, in one combined horrific deadly blast. That would turn the armor-plated VIP vehicle, alongside Abu Jabbar's Humvee, into a burning twisted hulk. Would vaporize their targeted most-wanted American, in a giant fireball.

"That will give the American kafir infidel a taste of hell, and send our precious martyr, to paradise, with rivers of milk and honey," the holy man gestured with exuberance.

"Who will drive Abu Jabbar's Humvee?" Sami hoped that they had found a more deserving martyr than himself. The cleric recited Sami's super qualifications, from US military experience, language, to his ID, despite the identification having been doctored. Who else could slip in, with Abu Jabbar's Humvee, alongside such a VIP military vehicle, Mullah asked, adjusting his headgear. "I am not deserving of such a great honor," Sami pleaded, hoping he could wiggle out of this horrendous task. Mullah Ahmad assured Sami, there was no greater Muslim to do Allah's will, than the conqueror of the crusader king--that heretical Pope.

His assignment flooded his brain with questions: where was Abu Jabbar's Humvee now? How would Sami know which vehicle was carrying the important American? Where and how he would receive the signal to join the VIP convoy? Would he not arouse suspicion, upon joining the procession? and many more unanswered questions that irked him.

The cleric replied with one word: patience. Ghazi Al-Muslawi, Sami's next contact, was in charge of those details, and had all his answers. This concluded Mullah Ahmad's briefing at the Al-Rasheed room. Next, he was to smuggle Sami out of the hotel, and deliver him to Ghazi, at Talal Shakir's warehouse. Later, Hassan, as the guest of record, would phone Al-Rasheed's front desk, informing them that he had checked out.

At the warehouse, Sami and Mullah Ahmad were met at the door by Ghazi himself. The cleric excused himself and left, leaving Sami with Al-Muslawi. His new host wore a white dishdasha dress and a checkered kaffiyeh. Sporting a goatee and a moustache, he kissed Sami on both cheeks, then escorted him to a corner apartment, pacing in open, floppy slippers. His host's bad toenails indicated, to Sami, unhealthy nutrition. Strange, irrelevant matters, flooded Sami's mind, in times of danger. Perhaps it was his desperate way to escape reality.

"Are you from Mosul? Isn't that what Muslawi means?" Sami was trying hard, not to think about his suicide scheme, due to unveil the following day. Ghazi smiled wistfully and explained that his father was from Mosul, but his mother hailed from heroic

Fallujah, as he put it. His childhood was spent in Mosul. He still had fond memories of that northern, mostly Arab Sunni city. It also boasted a sizable Kurdish population. As a kid, Al-Muslawi remembered wearing Arab garb, like his dad, and helping him at work, where his father was a reputed lumber merchant. This time, he bargained with a Kurd, who was in traditional baggy pants and a turban. The Kurdish man was selling poplar trees, grown near Zakho. Sami perked up, thinking about Hassan. "Did you like the Kurds?" Sami was itching to know.

"I lived in a mixed neighborhood, went to school with them; a buddy of mine was Kurdish. Like all people, there were good and bad ones amongst them," said Al-Muslawi. A sigh of relief came over Sami, knowing that no harm would come to Hassan, for his mere ethnicity, if he should meet these people.

Chapter 45--Execution Details

GHAZI AL-MUSLAWI, AL QAEDA'S nuts-and-bolts man, began implementing the scheme to kill the VIP. They believed him to be the US President himself--due to arrive the next day, Sunday. He pulled up a chair for Sami, in front of a small blackboard, that rested on an easel. Waving a pointer stick in his hand, he apologized for falling into his old habit of the teacher he used to be, in Fallujah. It was the only way he knew how to simplify complicated matters. More importantly, all this deathly secret information would be erasable on the blackboard. There would be no damning papers to carry around, Ghazi explained. Chalk in hand, he drew lines and sketched areas on the board. Baghdad International airport, the main highway to town, underground tunnel, the warehouse, and Sami's current location, all appeared closer to scale, than prior versions. Right then, a big fly landed on the board, just where he was about to write. In a huff, Al-Muslawi pulled his foot out of a slipper. He bent over, grabbed the footwear, and struck the fly dead with it. Ghazi then scraped off the mess with the slipper, dropped the footwear on the floor, and stepped back into it. He then continued, like nothing happened.

A new spot was marked on the airport road. It was about a hundred yards from the tunnel's intersection with the highway, in the direction of the airport.

"Abu Jabbar's Humvee is sitting here, waiting for you," smiled Ghazi, like a research professor announcing a breakthrough. Sami wiggled uncomfortably in his chair, then asked why it would not arouse suspicion. "Ah, I knew you would say that," grinned Al-Muslawi. "I can't wait to reveal all the precautions we've taken, to ensure our success and your worthy martyrdom," said Ghazi, moving the stick authoritatively. "You see, your Humvee, here, is not out in the open. It is inside a large square hole, which is deeper than the vehicle. The chamber is totally hidden, thanks to the cover of two large trap-doors, above the Humvee." Al-Muslawi took a sip of tea from his istikan cup. "These hinged ceiling covers can be pushed up, to open from inside. From outside, they are painted, to blend with the immediate surroundings." He looked triumphantly at Sami. "This had been carefully engineered and built by Talal Shakir. He had also planted trees and shrubs, to form a thicket around the big hole". Ghazi pointed at the secret passageway from the hidden vehicle chamber to the tunnel, which lead all the way to the warehouse, without venturing outside.

"A signal inside Abu Jabbar's vehicle triggers a double explosion--under the airport road, and above, in the Humvee," said Ghazi. "Remember, nothing happens until you drive over that hell-and-fire room, beneath the highway," he emphasized, in his professorial fashion.

Al-Muslawsi grabbed a flashlight and told Sami to follow him. After a long walk in the dark tunnel, they came face to face with a wooden wall.

"That's the powder room, under the main traffic," smirked Ghazi, recalling women's restrooms in old Hollywood movies; "they just finished stuffing it with high explosives. Even a tank will snap in two," he picked up a stick, and broke it in two, "just like this," Ghazi smiled, his white teeth glistening in the light of the flash. Suddenly, he took a sharp right turn into another tunnel. It ran along the side of the highway, leading into Abu Jabbar's Humvee, in its square-hole hideout. From outside, it was indistinguishable from similar military vehicles in the expected convoy to guard the American VIP. The vehicle lights stayed off, to avoid reflections exiting through the chamber's observation window. This was located below the hideout's overhead trap doors. Ghazi pointed out the exact blasting area, inside the Humvee, emphasizing all the safety precautions required of Sami, to avoid a premature martyrdom. "You get fewer houris that way," he quipped to a solemn Sami. He feigned a smile. The spotlight caught a pair of binoculars as well as night-vision goggles, in a plastic bag, inside a compartment. Carefully picking them up, he cleaned the lenses and handed them to Sami. "They are the best we could find, and you must have them handy tomorrow, so you can do your part exactly right. There's no room for even a single mistake." Ghazi used the goggles to try spotting an intended car, from the ceiling's observation window. To accurately hone in on a practice target, he peered through the powerful binoculars. "Here, look," said Al-Muslawi.

It was early twilight. Through the grove trees, Sami discerned airport traffic, with the sharp lenses, as it stretched over a mile. Passenger faces were so sharp and clear, that he swore he could have recognized Ghazi, if he was driving there. One car had a little Quran on top of its aerial. Sami relayed it to Al-Muslawi, who instantly declared that Allah had already set a place for them in paradise.

"Concentrate on military vehicles, tomorrow." Ghazi locked in a close-up onto the traffic. "Instead of the Holy Quran, find an eagle icon, on the tip of an aerial." He looked confidently at a puzzled Sami. "That one, will be the vehicle of the American VIP, our agent swears by Allah. Do you know why?" asked Al-Muslawi, reverting to the teacher mode. Sami shrugged in ignorance of it. "The eagle figurine was attached to the aerial's tip by the CIA, to instantly identify the guarded vehicle, in case of an emergency. Top secret information," declared Al-Muslawi, with the smirk of imminent achievement lighting up his face. This peak-value American, according to their Al Qaeda mole, would arrive at dawn, whose early light was comparable to the current dusk. Plus, the rising sun would sharpen Sami's lens-bound vision. This contrasted with their current binoculars' testing, at dusk, in which image clarity went down with the sun. After that, he showed Sami how to unlatch the upper trap doors, and flip them open using a long metal bar. This would be done the instant Sami could identify the eagle symbol on the military vehicle, at sunrise or before.

Like a good lecturer, Ghazi Al-Muslawi repeated the military-style drill three more times, covering every detail of tomorrow's operation. He paused for questions, after every round. Certain that Sami was up to the task, Ghazi lead him back to the house for evening prayers, a good dinner and plenty of rest.

Chapter 46--The Rendezvous

AT THREE, ON THIS fateful Sunday morning, Ghazi awakened Sami. He had been snoring on a sleeper ottoman, in Al-Muslawi's living room. While Sami washed, Ghazi rolled up the mattress, and stood in a corner. He pushed the bed into the lower section, then pulled down the upper half, turning it into one large, whole ottoman. After the Islamic ablutions, they performed early pre-dawn prayers. Then both ate a traditional breakfast, prepared by Ghazi. It featured omelet of basterma, consisting of minced spicy meat; there was also geymar, a thick, near-solid cream from water-buffalo milk. There was also yogurt and hot summoon, the oval-shaped Baghdad bread, that Iraqis go gaga over. After packing a few sandwiches, Ghazi handed Sami an AK-47 assault rifle, a machine gun, an alarm clock, and a bottle of water. He beckoned Sami, and headed for the door. Sami hesitated a little, then followed him to the suicide Humvee.

"If our missile gets that American's plane, at the airport, I'll rush over here, to inform you and ensure your escape. It's not smart to use traceable cellphoness." Ghazi then blessed Sami, and recited from Quran's Fatha chapter, the ritual that's performed at Muslim funerals, when the dead is usually in one piece. He kissed Sami on both cheeks twice. Ghazi then trekked through the two tunnel legs, back to his apartment. There he would await news of the US Satan's death, and Sami's martyrdom.

The alarm clock interrupted Sami's snooze in the cramped Humvee. He snapped back into deadly reality. Feeling hungry, he gobbled up his sandwich, then washed it down with a few gulps of water from the bottle. Just then, the pitch-darkness of the sky began to lighten up, heralding the dawn of a momentous day. US Air Force Colonel Sami Yusuf raised the high-powered, sharp-vision binoculars to his eyes. He peered through the small glass window, above ground level, just below the upper trap doors of the square chamber. They were hiding him and the killer Humvee. Traffic was minimal due to a curfew, which made Sami's task much easier. Any large-scale distant traffic noise would alert him to the long-awaited convoy, with the marked military vehicle. Unless, of course, Al Qaeda's Stinger missile would hit the high-flying plane, as it dived down for a landing, at Baghdad International airport.

Like the precise military man that he was, Colonel Yusuf went through his checklist one final time. He turned on the Humvee engine, tried the gears, brakes, doors, and any conceivable item that could go wrong, and foil his own personal scheme. "All systems go," he mumbled, as though he still was a US Air Force pilot. It all took a few minutes. He then turned the engine off, before exhaust fumes filled the outer chamber, and seeped into the Humvee. Sami then tested the rod, pushing up on the trap doors, covering the square hole that housed his vehicle. It worked fine, despite the creaky hinges. During all that, there was no sound of distant traffic, to alert him to his task.

Soon, he was behind the binoculars, and visibility was adequate, being somewhere between dawn and sunrise. There was a faraway rumble. A faint movement could be detected in the lenses, that seemed glued to Sami's eyes. Two motor cycles came into clear view, as they noisily lead a convoy. Then Sami saw an eagle figurine atop the antenna of the third vehicle, which he recognized as an MRAP vehicle, the new Mine Resistant Ambush Protected version of the Humvee. Air Force Colonel Yusuf recognized his Commander-In-Chief in the front passenger seat of this formidable Humvee. He also knew, that every living human inside had as much of a chance to survive as an ice cube in hell.

"Dogs, sons of dogs! Al Qaeda butchers of women and children! They want me to kill the President of the United States! The one I voted for!" Sami's reference to dogs, in the Iraqi dialect, was much stronger than sons-of-bitches in the American jargon. Without a moment to lose, he started his own fast-track procedure. The overhead trap doors were instantly pushed open, as he started the engine of the explosive-packed vehicle. In no time, the Humvee was out of the dugout, and on the highway, quickly approaching the roadside twin flags, which marked the underground explosives. This was a departure from Abu Jabbar's plan, which required Sami to wait for the VIP vehicle, then merge alongside it, as both Humvees drove past the two flags, over the buried dynamite. That would trigger simultaneous blasts in both, Sami's vehicle as well as the roomful of dynamite, buried under his Humvee. That would incinerate the highly-prized targeted American, as well as vaporizing Sami into Al Qaeda's Hall of Martyrdom.

About a hundred yards before the pair of flags, planted on imminent hell, Sami could see the convoy, in his rearview mirror, fast approaching him. He shifted into cruise control at a safe fifteen miles per hour, opened the vehicle door, then jumped out on the road's soft shoulder. Quickly, Sami got up and ran towards the convoy, waving his arms in the Air Force sign of 'STOP', as when guiding landing aircraft. Just when the lead police car swerved to a halt, to arrest Sami, a gigantic explosion lit up the sky, buffeting the presidential Humvee, before a huge newly-formed crater. The convoy passengers, all instantly hunkered down. Those outside, just jumped into ditches and nearby ground recesses. As soon as the cloud of dust and debris blew away, Sami got up and hurried to Al Qaeda's targeted VIP, waving a white handkerchief, to signify his peaceful intentions to the fast-approaching security personnel. Before arresting Colonel Yusuf, the President asked the guards to hold off and let the Iraqi American have his say.

"Air Force Colonel Sami Yusuf reporting for duty, Mr. President," Sami saluted in that unmistakable US military style.

The president returned the greeting in kind, highly pleased that a catastrophe was averted by this man. Consulting with his advisors, seated within beckon distance, the American commander in chief turned back to Sami.

"Colonel Yusuf, I'm very grateful for what you just did." The President looked relieved and almost smiling, though he tried hard to appear serious. "I'm in a dilemma. You killed the Pope then saved my life, all this while AWOL." He consulted once more with some expert inside. He gestured at Sami to come closer. "We have to place you under arrest, for alleged murder of the Pope," the President declared loudly. He then whispered to Sami: "When the whole legal process is over, I may grant you a pardon, if you can keep a secret."

In no time, the American and Iraqi heads of security were flanking Sami.

"This is American Air Force Colonel Sami Yusuf," said the US President to the two-nation security chiefs. "He is wanted by our military and the Italian authorities in the case of the deceased Holy Father." The President turned to his catholic advisor, who nodded his approval. He then looked at Sami. "Colonel, I order you to cooperate with our military and the Iraqi authorities, to facilitate your extradition to the United States, to stand trial," the President's voice broke.

"Yes Sir, Mr. President." The Iraqi American officer saluted, trying to suppress a smile.